Mr. Rude

Elizabeth Griff

Contents

Chapter 1

Scarlett's POV

Only 1 week left for my graduation.

I hope you don't fail

Be positive.

Finally I'm going to complete my graduation and I'm so much happy that now I can live my life according to my own rule.

Like my life my rules?

Kind of.

My mom would be so happy to know that I finally completed my graduation, she'll be head over heels to see me achieving my goal.

Why? Your mom don't trust you that you can be graduated?

Oh shut up!

I want to open my own boutique just like my mom and now after completing my graduation I can fulfil my dreams.

First let me introduce myself.I am a normal girl with brown hair, blue eyes, pale skin, around 5'5" with lil bit of curves on the right places. I also have two besties, one is Sonya and other is Richard.

Sonya is like my sister that I never got, she is so beautiful with dark brown hair and brown eyes with a very sexy figure, olive skin and around 5'6" height. she is every guys dream and not to forget my another best friend Richard aka Richie, who is a total drool worthy guy, every girl in our college tried to get his attention. He is about 6'1 and have light brown eyes, dark brown hair which looks sexy on him. He is such a flirt. How the girls get mad whenever he give them his toothy smile.

God I want a smile like him.

Hah! You wish

And not to forget my stupid inner voice who speaks more than me.

Oh you're jealous.

Of you? Sure.

All of us study in same college and now we are getting graduated. We are discussing about the party which is going to held after our graduation ceremony, yet I still can't decide what should I wear for the party. Dressing up is not an easy task. But, no problem as long as I'm having my besties with me I know I'll not face any problem.

Yeah! If you have to dress on your own I'm sure you'll be the clown roaming around the party.

Aaarrrrggghhh! Shut up.

Anyways, after attending all my classes for the day I was heading back home when from nowhere a guy came and bumped into me and the guy's phone fell down from his hand. I fell back on my butt but the guy made no attempt in helping me.

I groaned in pain.

I hope his phone is fine.

Hey! You should support me.

"Shit" He cursed under his breath while picking up his phone.

"Sorry" I apologized.

"You should be" he stated looking at his phone for any damage.

What? Did I hear it correct?

"What?" I asked him little bit surprised by his reply.

When he made eye contact with me I froze on my spot. He's totally a greek god. Wow!! With green eyes and height that is making me feel like a dwarf, perfectly sculpted jaw and not to forget his dark brown soft and silky hair. He's wearing a blue tux with white crisp shirt beneath. I can see the muscles clenching when he is moving his hands. He was so handsome, totally drool worthy guy.

Omg!! He's so hot and sexy. God had made him in free time.

I gulped.

After staring at him like a dumb person for sometime I came back to my senses and realised that I was drooling over him. I flushed at the thought of staring at him. He was saying something but I couldn't get it.

"Huh" I asked dumbly.

"I'm saying if you have done ogling me then you should say sorry to me as you bumped into me."

Busted. Wait he's saying you should say sorry?

Is he for real? I was about to give him a piece of mind but he cut me off in the mid.

"Don't you have eyes or your eyes are only for drooling over boys" he smirked, looking at me or more like judging me.

He's so full of himself. God! Scarlett my soldier tell him that he can't insult you like that.

I nodded.

"Who the hell you think you are, talking to me like that" I huffed. He's the one who bumped into me and now he's blaming me. How can be a person so arrogant.

Yupp. Sexy arrogant person.

I know, but

Hey! Don't praise him.

Oh! Sexy arrogant person whom I cannot praise.

I groaned.

"You know what, forget it, you already wasted a lot of my time, I don't wanna waste any more. So, now move" he said in annoyance.

Like hell I would let him go like that.

I didn't move and crossed my arms showing him that I'm not going anywhere but he just pushed me aside and carried on his way just ignoring me like he can't even see me.

Who the bloody hell was he? I know you are Scarlett but he shouldn't treat you like this.

Exactly!

He kept moving on without even giving a second glance at me.

I stomped my feet at his arrogance, how I wish to remove that bloody smirk from his face.

What was this guy's problem. He can't even apologize for a single thing which he did wrong.

I groaned in annoyance.

He's seriously so rude.

MR. RUDE.

Seriously God why do you have to make such freak and arrogant people?

I hope that this is our first and last meet, and we never meet again. I wish I stay away from this Mr. Rude guy.

After all that complaining I started walking back towards my house.

Chapter 2

Scarlett's pic above... what do you guys think??

Guys if you don't like her, you can use your own imagination.

Scarlett's POV

It's been a week since I bumped into that Mr. Rude guy.

I hope I never meet that guy again.

I'm happy that I haven't crossed paths with him again.

Liar. You're dying to meet him.

Why would I be dying?

Aren't you the one thinking about him all the time?

Yeah! He got some nice looks and that body plus those eyes, but that doesn't mean I would forget his impolite behavior.

Sure. Why not.

Let's forget about him and lemme enjoy today's day. Today is our graduation ceremony and our college has invited the most famous bachelor Mr. Eros Jordan, Ceo of the Jordan Trades and Co., afterwards there will be a graduation party for all the graduates. I'm too excited for the party.

I came to know a little about the ceo guy, Mr. Eros Jordan. He's so handsome and sexy. He's every girls dream and not to forget the arrogance, rudeness and attitude with his charming looks. But he has achieved a lot in lesser time, which made me a lil bit excited to know more about him.

Why can't the handsome and rich guys be sweet and polite? Why are they so arrogant? So full of themselves?

You have a point there but, why would I care, I don't want any arrogant guy in my life.

Wow! Our Scarlett rhymed a line.Amazing.

I rolled my eyes.

I'm really very excited to finally get my degree. Yippiee.

Now, I'm getting ready for the party with Sonya. I want to wear my brown dress but Sonya said that I'll look like a nerd in that because of its simplicity but I don't think so. Hey! don't you all dare think that I'm a nerd, because I'm not but Sonya is a fashion queen so she thinks I dress up like a nerd plus I have a like for books too, may be that made her think of me like that. Nevermind, now I'm wearing a royal blue dress which reaches my mid thigh, with sweetheart neckline. I let my hair down, with a minimal amount of makeup done by Sonya and not to forget my heels. I love my heels a lot. I usually don't like getting ready that much. I'm more of a pajama kinda girl. What a comfort they give. But a girl have to get ready sometimes, so let it be. When I was done I took a glance of myself in the mirror,

I gasped, Sonya really did a work on me, the girl in the mirror look stunning.

Are you sure you're the same girl in the mirror?

I'm confused too.

"Someone's going to be in the spot light" Sonya teased.

I blushed.

When I looked towards Sonya, she is looking fab with her red strapless dress and with those black killer heels she looked sexy.

"God Sonya you look sexy" I complimented.

"I know babes" she said with a wink.

"Now, lets go, we're getting late." she said. With that we left our house and reached our soon to be ex-college.

As we reached Scarlett ran off to his boyfriend, leaving me alone. Why Sonya why?

When I was about to enter my soon to be ex-college, I ran into a wall.

From where did this wall come?

Seriously Scarlett? You can't even see the Walls? Atleast leave the poor walls. What if they break someday?

Shut up!

Due to the collision I was about to fall on my butt two strong arms grabbed my waist and helped me in regaining my posture.

Hey it is not a wall. Shit it's not a wall but a chest. A very muscular chest.

Why do you always keep on bumping in the people? Why are you so clumsy?

"Sorry" I said.

But when I raised my eyes to see the face I was shocked. Shock would be an understatement. I was standing still in my place. Familiar green eyes came in my view. Damn! He's the same guy I bumped into a week ago. The same guy I was dream- Uh, nothing.

Really? You can't bump into another guy? Why him?

He's staring me with a gaze I don't know but when he recognizes me.

"Not you again" he huffed.

Oh!! Now he's awake.

"Why the hell you keep on bumping me? I seriously think you should consult a doctor for your eyes" he annoyingly said.

What the hell is his problem?

"Yupp it's me and Thanks for your stupid advice for which I don't give a shit. Keep your stupid advice to yourself" he narrowed his eyes at me.

Scar - 1Mr. Rude - 0

"Why is a freak like him is allowed in our college?" I muttered to myself.

"What?" he questioned.

"Nothing of your concern, now get away from my way as I'm not interested in talking to you. Now move" I said, by pushing him aside I carried on my way.

Bravo!

Scar - 02Mr. Rude - 00

I grinned.

When I turned around after walking some distance he was no more standing there. I ignored him and entered in my soon to be ex-college.

At the entrance I saw a familiar face waving towards me. Ain't he so sexy?

Stupid. He's Richie.

Ohh!

My bestie Richie. He was standing there in formal wear. He's looking dashing as always. I hugged him when I reached close to him.

"Wow, someone is looking hot" I said with a wink.

He smiled with his sexy smile.

"Not too bad yourself. I never knew that you are so sexy otherwise I would surely had tried on you" he said with a wink.

I blushed.

"Oh shut up" I smacked his arm.

"Where's Sonya?" he asked.

"With Joel(Sonya's boyfriend)... her pumpkin" I laughed which soon he joined.

Afterwards we went to the hall where the ceremony was going to be held. We got seated on our allotted seats and soon Sonya joined us with his pumkin, holding their hands. They make such a cute couple.

Yeah! A girl with a fat vegetable.

Joel is a hansome looking guy with grey eyes and black hair and height around 5'9". He gives an aura of a bad boy. But he's perfect for her as he can handle someone like Sonya. Sonya and Joel were dating for a few months. But they make a cute couple. I adore them a lot.

Soon the sound of microphone echoed in the hall and our professor started his rather boring speech. He introduced the chief guests. Soon I heard the name of Mr. Eros Jordan. When I looked at the stage I froze on my spot.

Nooo.. it can't be happening.

He's the same guy with green eyes.

Into whom I'm keep bumping.

Who is,

None other than.

Mr. Rude.

Oh God! Kill me now.

Chapter 3

E ros's pic above

Scarlett's POV:

Seriously, him again, and he's the infamous Eros Jordan.

Scar why did you bump into the billionaire. I think the wall would have been better.

First time in my life I agree with you.

As he came on the stage the crowd loudly applauded for him, and that's when he showed his signature smile. His smile is wow. He was wearing royal blue tux and he was totally looking like a Greek God in all those lightings.

But still he's the same Mr. Rude don't forget that.

My inner voice reminded me.

Girls were literally drooling over him. I can see the girls how they are focusing on him only.

When he was seated at one of the seats for the guests he started looking in the crowd. I hid my face under my hand but still he noticed me and smirked his evil smirk.

I am sure that he was smirking at my way only. He was watching me with such a great intensity.

I shuddered.

"Ohh look he's smiling at me" a girl behind me said.

I stopped the urge to laugh.

"No dumbo. He's looking at me. Look carefully." another girl said.

But I know to whom he was showing his smirk.

I tried to stick to the seat and not to run like a caveman out of the hall.

Why me?

Now the great Eros Jordan started his speech as our head invited him to do so, and I'm having a strange feeling that he's looking at my side only.

Soon distribution of degrees started.

Sonya tapped my shoulder and asked "I don't know why but kinda feel like the hot guy is staring at you?"

Because he is.

"Yes he is, because he's the same guy into whom I bumped." I annoyingly said.

She gasped "Omg! Don't tell me you bumped into the most sexiest bachelor Eros Jordan. You are such a lucky girl. I think I should also start bumping into random people" she said.

If only she knew.

I hushed her as my turn to collect my degree came. I got up from my seat and Sonya and Richie wished me luck. As I reached the stage Eros smirked his dangerous smirk at me. I flushed and nervously reached in front of him and when I was standing in front of him to collect my degree he shook his hand with me and squeezed it.

He smiled.

"Congratulations Scarlett....babe"

What??

He said babe...huh?

My eyes widen.

I snatched my hand from his grip and glared at him.

But he winked at me.

I got dumbfounded. Did he just wink at me or was it my imagination? I can feel the heat reaching my cheeks and I know my face was red from the embarrassment.

He chuckled at my situation.

Oh Mother Earth open up and swallow me, please.

Within no time I quickly walked from the stage and ran from there.

When I came away from there I released my breath which I don't know I was holding. My heart was beating like hell.

What the hell just happened?

After flowing some colourful words from my mouth for that arrogant but hot Mr.Rude. I walked back towards the area where the party will happen.

He must have gone by now. No need to worry.

As soon as I reached there I spotted my friends standing there.

"Hey guys" I said taking a fruit punch as I was feeling thirsty.

"Where the heck were you? You weren't answering your calls? Are you out of your freaking mind? You just walked away from the hall without telling us about your where abouts?" Sonya yelled.

"Exaclty Scar are you insane? We were worried about you. You should have told us where were you going." this is Richie.

"Calm down you guys. I'm okay and I'm not a kid. You know I'm a graduated girl" I winked at both.

Bad moment for your humor.

They both annoyingly roll their eyes.

I chuckled.

"Now forget everything lets party. Don't be a party pooper" I requested.

"Okay. Lets party" said Richie cheerfully.

He grabbed both my and Sonya's hand and dragged us to the dance floor.

We danced like there is no tomorrow.

"Guys, I'm going to rest for a while. My feets are killing me" I said.

"Me too. These killer heels" said Sonya.

As we both got seated I noticed Sonya is looking me in a different way.

I think something ugly is on your face.

What?

Your face.

That was so bad.

"What?" I asked Sonya.

"You know after you ran out from the hall the hot guy asked me about you" she said.

What??

"W-who?" I stuttered.

"The Eros guy. What's going on?" She teased.

"Nothing. There is nothing between us. He's such a stupid conceited guy. Who don't know how to apologize for his mistakes and doesn't even care for anyone, jerk" I stated.

"Wow in few meets you learnt a lot about him.. nice" she winked.

"Shut up" I said.

"I don't wanna talk about him. Forget about him and I'm not going to meet him again. Anyways, how's your pumpkin and where is he?" I questioned to change the subject.

No more Mr.Rude talks.

"Okay. As you say. Pumpkin went home as his mother was not feeling well. I asked him if he need me he said he'll manage" she said.

"You know you both are perfect for each other. I wish I could find a guy who would be perfect for me" I said dreamingly.

"Soon you'll get your perfect match babe. Now let's enjoy and rescue our friend from those clingy girls" she laughed.

Then we both went to Richie and helped our poor friend.

We partied till late night. Richie dropped me at my home and soon I wore my comfy clothes and jumped on my bed with my teddy baby.

Today's thoughts came in my mind.

I hope I never meet that guy again.

Another chapter done.Pheeww...I hope you guys love the chapter.

Love y'all

18/03/2018

Chapter 4

R ichie's pic above

All new POV for all of you.Enjoy

Eros's POV

After attending the meeting and cracking the deal with Mr. Watson. I was very happy that I cracked this deal. My rival company wanted this deal but me being me, won't let that happen.

After all you're the famous Eros Jordan.

Thank you thank you.

Seriously?

I was totally exhausted and moving back to my penthouse but suddenly my phone started ringing, and the caller was my secretary. I picked it up.

"Yes Maya" I asked.

"Sir, there is a graduation ceremony in Trinity college in which your presence is requested." she said.

"And when is this ceremony happening?" I questioned.

"Next week Sir and there are no other meetings on that day. Would you be able to go?" she asked.

Means you have to attend that function.

While talking to Maya suddenly a girl came and bumped into me and she fell on her butt, and due to bumping my phone also fell down. I cursed under my breath "Shit".

Where the hell was she watching while walking?

The girl got up while rubbing her butt and brushing dust from her clothes."Sorry" she said.

"You should be" I huffed without looking at her. I was in no mood to talk and it's all her fault why didn't she moved away when she saw me coming.

You were also not seeing where are you going.

My inner voice said.

I know but I'm not going to apologise. I'm the Ceo I don't apologise to anyone.

"What?" She asked shockingly.

Is she deaf? Can't she hear it in first time?

When she looked up our eyes met.

Wow. She's so beautiful.

She had sparkling blue eyes, her hair were brown, pale skin, full lips, her whole look screams innocence. She's a true beauty.

But she's also the one who bumped into you. My inner voice reminded me.

Bad timing.

I regained my posture and started blaming her.

Why do I take all the blame on me?

"Huh" she asked.

Oh man! She was checking you out.

I repeated myself after clearing my throat.

When she didn't replied I contined accusing her.

After wasting some time with the stupid argument with her.

I pushed her aside and kept moving on with shooting daggers on her side.

She yelled at me. But I ignored her and continued on walking on my way.

When I turned around she was standing there still shocked.

I smiled to myself.

She's cute I hope I meet her soon.

---****----

It's been a week since I bumped into that girl. I never saw or bumped into her again. She was so innocent from her looks what would be she like from inside? I really wanna know her.

I sighed.

I wish I could meet her again.

Man you're whipped.

Shut up. I don't have feelings for her. I have met her only once. And it was not a proper meeting.

Today is that graduation ceremony in Trinity college and I'm on my way to the college.

When I entered the college, I was walking inside when I suddenly bumped into someone, and that someone was about to fall I grabbed her waist as soon as I came to know that someone is she and when she lift up her face, same sparkling blue eyes. Yes, I mean no, she's that girl to whom I keep bumping. She's looking sexy in her royal blue dress but still looking cute and soon I came to know I am checking her out.

We are kind of matching.

You're so happy to see her. Totally whipped.

"Not you again" I huffed.

Fake acting.

I'm not acting.

Everyone knows.

"Why the hell you keep on bumping me. I seriously think you should consult a doctor for your eyes" I said.

I know this will make her furious. I grinned to myself.

Now tell I'm whipped or not.

Yupp.Totally whipped.

I groaned.

After a small argument she walked away from me. But this time by pushing me aside.

Not so innocent. She's fiesty, but I like it.

Then the head of the college came and I walked away in with him.

But what was she doing here?

Don't know.

After sometime when I have to enter in the area where ceremony is happening, a large crowd came into my view. Who were hooting and shouting. I just gave them a smile and got seated to my alloted seat.

Let's get over with it.

I was looking in the crowd when someone catches my attention. Who is none other than that bumping girl. She was hiding her face under her hand, her gesture made me smirk.

She thinks that she'll hide herself from this whipped man's gaze. She's so wrong.

Hey! I'm not whipped.

Afterwards I gave a speech on my business by looking at her side only. She's talking to a girl sitting beside her and a guy next to her. Is he her boyfriend?? I shaked my head and ignored all the thoughts and concentrated on my speech which was written by me. liar.

My inner voice scolded.

Okay... it was written by my secretary Maya... happy?

You can't even think.My inner voice teased.

Soon the degree distribution started and one by one students came.

Then Scarlett Miller's name announced and the bumping girl came. ohh bumping girl has a name... I chuckled.

With the looks of her she was nervous and I know somewhere it is because of me. I smirked.

She came in front of me. I gave the degree to her and shaked my hand with her giving a little squeeze.

She flushed.

"Congratulations Scarlett... Babe" I said with a wink.

Her face became scarlett red just like her name. She was blushing... because of you.

My inner voice said.

I smiled a genuine smile..

She snatched his hand from me and quickly walked away from there.

I chuckled at her cuteness.

After distributing all the degrees my eyes were searching for that blue one, but I can't find her.

Then I saw that girl who was talking to her in the ceremony.I approached her.

"Have you seen Scarlett?" I asked.

She shaked her head and said " I'm also looking for her whenI'll find her I'll surely tell her that you were asking for her". She smiled.

I nodded and walked away.

I thought I'll talk to her this time, but,

No problem.

Better luck next time.

Yeah.

With that I headed towards my penthouse as I am in no mood of working.

Yeah! You want alone time for your bumping girl's thoughts.

After reaching my penthouse I freshen myself and wore my sweatpants and lie down on my bed and closed my eyes.

Blue eyes came into my view,

Her name is Scarlett, it totally suits her.

"I hope I'll meet you soon, Scarlett" I said.

With that I fall into a deep sleep.

Another chapter done...I hope you guys like our star of the story's POV... if you find any problem do tell me...

Love y'all guys

18/03/2018

Chapter 5

S onya's pic above...What do you think??

Scarlett's POV

It's been two weeks since graduation and I was looking further to get some coaching related to fashion designing.

After fully wasting two weeks sitting at home doing nothing, today Sonya and I planned to go for our favourite thing.

Shopping

I love shopping. Isn't it amazing to buy new dresses, accessories, make-up and heels, how can I forget them.

They are true love.

So we both are going to the nearby mall as they have a very good collection of dresses.

I was wearing a beige coloured jumpsuit with black heels. My hairs in are tied in a messy bun, mascara and lip gloss. I don't like to be covered in make up all the time.

After getting a final glimpse of myself in mirror. When I was picking up my purse I heard sound of a car honking.

Sonya's here. Now let's do some shopping.

I hurriedly walked towards the door telling mom that I'm leaving. Sonya came into my view, sitting in her red Mercedes. She look hot as always.

I got seated in the passenger seat after hugging her and soon we were off to the mall.

As we reached the mall we firstly went to buy the dresses.

After trying dresses for uncountable times, I got exhausted. After buying dresses we decided to buy heels. Soon I felt more energetic.

I grinned.

Magic of heels.

I bought five pairs of heels, they were literally begging me to buy them and I can't listen them begging, so I bought them.

Heels were begging? Seriously?

My inner voice asked which I chose to ignore and kept on completing my shopping.

When we finally got exhausted we came to the food area to feed our poor tummy.

"One cold coffee and one ice tea and two blueberry muffins please" I ordered to the waiter with a smile.

Soon our orders came and we were gossiping, so we took a pause and started our eating continuing with our gossips.

After some gossiping we headed towards our home.

As I entered my home I felt something fishy was going on, maybe your mother is cooking fish. my inner voice joked.."very funny" I said to my inner voice.

"Scar... are you home?" My mum asked.

"Yes mom" I replied.

"Please come in my room I want to have a talk with you" mum said.

Why doesn't it sounds nice??

Same with me.

"Yes mom?" I asked. She was sitting on her bed. She was in some deep thoughts. I knocked the door to gain her attention. She looked at me.

"Have a seat" she said patting the space beside her. I walked towards her and sat beside her.

"So how was your shopping?" mum asked. "Good" I replied.

I have a feeling that your mom is about to burst a bomb on your head. I think you should wear helmet first.

"Shut up" I said to my inner voice.

"Honey? Are you listening?" Mum asked.

"Yeah, sorry mum.. uhh. .what were you saying?" I asked.

"Yes, so I was telling you that I met my best friend Carol yesterday. You know her right? My childhood friend?" mum asked.

I nodded.

"So she was asking about you and I told her that you just completed your graduation and now preparing for the further studies in fashion industry" mom is getting nervous. Is something wrong?

I bit my lip.

"So she asked me if.. uhh.. you... uhh... mmm...." mum stuttered.

"Yes mom? Is anything wrong? Are you alright?" I patiently questioned by squeezing her hand. "She asked me that she...ehh.. she wants you to marry her son and become her daughter in law" she said after which she released her breath.

What?

I told you. Now look a bomb bursted and you didn't use any protection. Now handle this new problem.

Nooo...Noooo...Noooooo.....

"Noooo" I yelled.

"No mom I can't and I won't marry someone like this" I stated. "Mom I'm 21.. just 21. I have my dreams ahead. A whole future ahead of me. I can't sacrifice my dreams for a marriage, nooo noo ,I won't marry any one, sorry to disappoint you mom but no, I won't marry anyone this soon. Please try to understand" I said still in shock.

"But honey it is best for you and you can fulfil your dream after marriage also and the guy whom you'll marry he's one the famous ceo. You'll be happy my dear. Please don't say no. You know I have very strong relationship with Carol. She's the only one for me who supported me after your dad's death. Your no will cost me my friendship and I don't want to loose my only friend. And I don't see anything bad in it." she said.

Yeah why would you she see something bad in it? She's not the one marrying an unknown guy.

I was standing there in shock, battling with myself. What should I do now? And this bloody inner voice always leaves me when I need her the most.

"Honey you know I'm getting old day by day and I don't know how much life is ahead of me, but before dying I want to see you happy. Don't I deserve this. I only want to see my daughter happy. Please baby please. Listen to me this time and I guarantee you that you won't regret this decision. Please Scarlett, please understand what I'm saying" she said with tear in her eyes.

I can't see her like this. I can't make her cry, after dad she's my only family. But I don't want to marry so soon. What should I do?

I can meet the guy and then make him say no to marry me. Yes. That would be perfect.

This is the best idea for now.

My mother is about to go I stopped her and hugged her and said "I'll marry him mom. I'll marry him. I'll marry whosoever you want me to marry I'll marry him"

She tightly hugged me and clapped her hands.

She smiled squealed like a kid.

"Okay honey I'll tell your soon to be mother-in-law about your acceptance" she smiled and kissed my forehead.

When she was leaving the room I heard her muttering yes. Was this her plan?

No. My mom is so sweet and innocent. She won't trick me.

Its time to think what should I do now?

Who knows may be that guy rejects you.

Your idea is not that bad. I have to convince that ceo guy to not to marry me, may be he was facing the same thing as me.

When I was leaving for my room for a good sleep I heard my mum "my daughter agreed. I know she can't see me cry. I used this against her. I know I know but this is for her own good" mum said while talking on the phone.

What the hell?

Exactly what the hell? My mum my innocent mom fooled me to say yes for this marriage.

Unbelievable

And I got fooled so easily. Damn. But who's gonna marry that guy.

I evilly smirked.

My mom is something else. I laughed at my mom's plan. She totally fooled me.

Now I have to meet that Ceo guy.

I came to my room and took a shower and wore something comfy and lied down on my bed.

Hey! I forgot to ask that ceo guy's name.

As I care about his name. Afterall I'm going to make him say no to me. I squealed in my mind and finally closed my eyes.

I hope that the guy don't find me beautiful.

Hello lovely readers...

Another chapter done...

Please do comment and vote for the story... so I'll know that you are liking it...

So what do you think what will happen...

To know keep on reading...

Love y'all guys...

19/03/2018

Chapter 6

Eros's POV

Two weeks have been passed when I last met Scarlett.

I smiled at her thought.

Even her name makes you smile. Exclusively whipped.

Shut up.

Today there was a meeting with Mr. Watson. It was kind of boring.

Kind of? Are you insane it was totally boring.

Okay.

I sighed and walked towards the conference room.

But soon it got finished. With a sigh I came back to my office after shaking hands with Mr. Watson.

After doing a few work I wrapped up my work and was ready to head back to my house.

I exited my office and walked towards my baby, my love, my black Audi A6 where my driver Jimmy was waiting for me.

"Good evening Sir " he greeted with a nod.

I nodded in reply.

I got seated in the back seat, afterwards Jimmy came to his seat and we were off to my house.

As I reached my house, while entering I saw an old lady sitting on the couch. She's your mom stupid. My inner voice scolded.

Oh!

"Hey Mom" I greeted her.

Bro something is not right. I can tell you.

Oh! shut up. You are exaggerating. Everytime my mom comes to meet me you always say that.

You don't trust me. I was with you all the time and now I'm facing this.

Such a drama queen.

I ignored my inner voice and concentrated on my mom.

"Hello my lovely son" she replied while hugging me.

See, she's calling you lovely. Bro you're still not believing me, right?

I chose to ignore him again.

"How was your work?" She asked while making herself comfortable on the couch.

"Good" I replied briefly.

Why did she come?

"Why are you here mom?" I asked.

She narrowed her eyes at me.

"Can't a mother come to meet her lovely son?" She replied.

Something is going to happen. Be ready.

Now I'm also getting the same feeling as you. I said to my inner voice.

"Yes mom you can, but at this time. Is something wrong?" I worriedly asked.

"Actually, I met my bestfriend today." she hesitated.

"That's good. What's the problem in that?" I asked.

"No dear, there is no problem" she nervously laughed.

"So? Is everything alright?" I again questioned her.

"Umm... I met her and as you know she is my best friend since childhood... um, as you are also getting older..umm, soo.. uhh..." she stuttered.

Your mom never stutters. Something is definitely wrong. I can't hear anymore. I'm going.My inner voice said.

She sighed then in a single go she said " I want you to marry her daughter." after saying she released her breath.

What?

Marry her daughter?

No way.

See, see, I told you she came here to get you married. I told you but you won't believe me.

I frowned.

Zip it up. No more words. Let me think.

"And why do you think that I'll marry her?" I questioned her and raised my eyebrow.

What was she thinking? That I'll gladly accept her proposal. I don't even know that girl, what if she was fat or what if she was ugly or some slut? Noo man! I can't see you like that, you have an image to maintain.

I sighed.

First time I agree with you.

"No mom I can't" I stated bluntly.

You are Eros Jordan. The most droolworthy bachelor alive. Girls are dying to be at your side and she thinks that you'll marry any girl, any unknown girl. No way. This is not gonna happen.

"Please son for your mum's sake please marry her. She's beautiful and well mannered. I had seen her and she is a perfect match for you. You'll definitely love her. She's so kind and sweet." she requests.

Say no to her. Say noo. Say N.O. NO. A very big no. You can marry any girl you want. Don't say yess otherwise I'll kick your ass.

Just say no to her.

"Yes mom, err... I mean no mom I won't marry any girl. Especially an unknown girl. I don't even know her mom, what if she's not kind as you're saying? What if she's a gold digger, you know I'm not a fan of gold digger, why are you forcing me mom?" I asked her.

"Son I'm not forcing you it's your life and what if she's the right girl for you? You should atleast meet her. Without meeting her you won't be able to know how perfect is she for you, You love you mum no? Please meet her, if you don't like her then I won't force you, pretty please" she said while showing her puppy eyes.

How will I say no to her.

Bro I think one meeting won't cost anything.. and then you can make the girl say no and your mum will stop forcing you and you'll enjoy you're life.

Umm..do you think so?

Yup

Okay then.

"Okay mum. I'll meet her but if I don't like her you'll never ever force me in life for marriage and you'll stop being the cupid for me. Okay?" I told her.

"Okay, my lovely son. I'll do whatever you say. I love you so much" she said while kissing me on the cheek.

"I'll soon prepare a meeting for you two and I know you are most definitely going to like her" she winked.

I meekly nodded with a sigh.

"Now I have some urgent works. I got to go, will meet you soon" she said while getting up with an ear to ear smile.

A victorious smile.

Your mom is a smart one, she knows how to make someone say yes.

I know.

"Okay honey, take good care of yourself. I will tell my friend that our plan worked. uhh.. I mean you're ready to meet her daughter " she smiled a nervous smile.

Huh?

What is my mum planning??

She started walking towards the door but suddenly stopped and turned around and said "By the way the girl's name is Scarlett"

What?

Scarlett?

Is she the same?

As I was about to ask her but the shutting of door's sound came and I knew she left.

I sighed.

Can she be the same girl?

May be or may be not. We don't know her full name yet.

I don't think so that she'll be that Scarlett.

You'll get to know when you'll meet the girl.

I reached the kitchen and eat my dinner which was made by my chef.

After eating, I reached my room and came out from my clothes and took a long hot shower and wore some comfortable clothes and lied down on my bed.

I put my hands under my head and started thinking to save myself from mom's proposal. I think I should make the girl hate me, may be she'll reject me.

But what if the girl is my Scarlett?

Seriously your Scarlett???

Yeah right. she's not mine.

Yet.

I sighed

And soon closed my eyes.

Within few minutes I was out.

Another chapter done...

So what do you think will happen when both of them meet...

Excited??

Then keep on reading and supporting...

Do tell me about your views...

Thank you for reading...

Love y'all guys....

19/03/2018

Chapter 7

Guys if you are liking my story... please do comment...

So.. I'll know that you are liking it...

Enjoy your reading..

Scarlett's POV

Its been two days since my mom bursted a giant bomb on me.

She didn't say anything after that and was busy in doing her work.

My mom has her own boutique. I got inspired from her and want to help her in future.

Aww, so sweet. Like mother like daughter.

I smiled.

I told all about the marriage news to my friends, both were like what the hell is your mom thinking, sudden marriage, you are so young for marriage, all these words are from Richie. It's really great to know that someone other than your family cares for you.

But when I told Sonya she said "wow, lucky you, marrying a ceo guy. Is he sexy? Is he tall? Babe I envy you. I wish I also had a mom like you." She is totally insane. Here I'm feeling sad that I'm getting married and she is saying all these things. But deep down I know she was saying all this to lift my mood.

I sighed.

I was in my room, busy in playing games in my phone when there's a knock on my door.

"It's open" I yelled.

The door opened and my mom's face came into my view. She was smiling. She came and sat beside me showing her cute smile.

Be ready girl.. my inner voice warned.

Ohh! hush up.

"Hey honey. How are you?" She asked politely.

Isn't she being very polite??

I ignored my inner voice.

"I'm fine mom. How about you?" I replied with a smile.

Smile as much as you can.

Can't you keep your mouth shut.

Okay. As you say, but babes you'll soon see, How evil your mom is?

I rolled my eyes.

"I'll surely be fine as my little baby girl is completing her mother's wish. Infact I'm not fine I'm on cloud nine to have such a daughter like you. I'm glad that you're my daughter" she smiled by showing her shiny teeth.

I smiled in reply.

"I talked to your future mother-in-law about the marriage and she told me that her son is also ready, so we decided to arrange a meeting for both of you." she cheerfully said.

See I told you to be ready.

You're right.

Now go and meet him and make him say no to you.

I secretly smiled at my inner voice.

"So you both are meeting tomorrow at The Chelsea's. Be ready and reach there by 12 noon. And here is a dress for you, which I specially made for my honey bunch" she said while handing me the box.

It was a white coloured box with pink ribbon knotted on the top of the box.

When I opened the box my eyes widen, it has an white dress with pearls embedded in its neck, it was so beautiful.

I'm in love it.

Me too.

I jumped from my seat and crushed my mum by tightly hugging her.

Time for revenge. Now it's time to crush your mum's bone.

"Thank you mum, thank you so much. This dress is soo beautiful. I love you I love you I love you so much" I said with a kiss on her cheek.

Thank God. At least something good is happening in all this drama.

I grinned.

"No problem baby. I'm glad you liked the dress. Be ready and reach there on time. Don't make him wait" she said happily.

"Don't fail me" she said warningly.With that she left by closing the door.

Hey.. you again forgot to ask the ceo guy's name.

Shit.

You should have told me before.

What can I say? I forgot, after all I'm your conscience.

I sighed.

I'll ask her in the morning.

I continued on my game.

----****----

Beep

Beep

Beep

I really want to kill the person who invented this sleep disturbing device, alarm clock.

I groaned and shutted the alarm off.

And burried my face in the pillow.

Get up. You sleepy ass. You have a man to reject.

Right.

But who the heck made this rule that we have to wake up in the morning. I hate mornings. Why mornings can't be in the evening?

I have an idea. Why don't you keep on sleeping then you don't have to meet that guy?

Brilliant idea.

I high fived my inner voice.

As I was about to sleep again my door opened and my mum started yelling.

Damn! I don't think she is gonna leave you.

"Wake up honey. You should start getting ready otherwise you'll be late. Get up. Get up quickly" she said by clapping her hands.

I hid my face more in the pillow.

Soon the noises stopped. I think my mum left my room.

I victoriously smiled.

I don't think the same. After all she's your mom.

I was about to open an eye to check on my surroundings but suddenly I heard a loud noise near my ear.

I screamed and fall off my bed with a loud thud.

I rubbed my now aching bums.

When I looked up, I saw my mum laughing at me with a phone in her hand. She made that loud sound from the phone.

I groaned in protest.

"Gotcha" she said laughingly.

"Now get ready" she chuckled and left my room to let me get ready.

I defeatedly got up from my bed and went to bathroom. After getting showered I looked the watch and its 11.

Shit! I'm going to be late.

Who wants to reach there on time?

Not me, but I have to otherwise I'll be dead.

I quickly wore my dress and let my hair fall down wore my nude heels. Applied little bit of gloss and with mascara I completed my look. I glanced at the mirror and after confirming my look I went down.

My mum was standing there " Honey, you're looking gorgeous" she said with a kiss on my forehead.

I was to about to leave when my inner voice reminded me.

Who'll you meet if you don't ask the guy's name.

Oh yeah, thanks.

"Mum? What's his name?" I asked.

"Ah! sorry dear I forgot to tell you, um.. his name is um... I forgot his first name. But his last name is something like Jordan. Sorry dear, but don't worry he knows your name and the bookings are already done, you'll find him" she said with a smile.

"Okay. I should be going now. Bye mom" I kissed her cheek and left her.

I took a taxi as I'm in no mood to drive.

Jordan, I have heard this name somewhere.

My train of thoughts got interrupted when the taxi driver told me that we've reached our destination.

I jumped out from the taxi and paid my fare to the taxi driver, and entered the restaurant.

I reached the reception and asked for the bookings under Mrs. Miller.

As I was about to move to where the receptionist told me that's when I bumped into a hard chest.

Crap! Not again.

"Sorry, it was my mistake." but when I looked up.

Noo way.

Noo freaking way.

Same pair of green eyes were looking at me.

Why you always end up bumping and specially into him?

He was staring at me with a confused gaze, his mouth is hung open. He's looking so sexy and hot in his casual wear, but wait can anyone tell me?

What is he doing here?

He's definitely stalking you.

I got frustrated and bluntly asked him "Are you bloody stalking me?"

"No. That's not my style babes but for you I can do it if you want" he winked.

I rolled my eyes.

"Then why are you always in the same place as me? If you are not stalking me?" I said while narrowing my eyes at him.

"I can say the same for you. You were also always there where I was and am" he smirked and crossed his arms over his chest and glanced me from up to down.

OMG! he's checking you out.

Pervert.

I shifted uncomfortably.

I pointed my index finger at him.

"You..." but I was cut off by a waiter.

"Mr. Jordan come with me. I'll show you your table." the waiter said to him and he was about to go when the bells of my mind rung.

Jordan? Doesn't this name rings a bell?

My eyes widen in shock.

Can he be the same.

I think he's the same.

Oh god no, please. Don't let this happen. Please make it a dream.

"And mam is there any chance that you are Scarlett Miller?" he asked.

I nodded.

"A table for both of you has been booked by Mrs. Miller, so come this way" the waiter said.

I froze after listening this.

Noooooooo.

This can't be true.

I'm surely dreaming.

Someone please pinch me.

I can kick you if you want.

Seriously why he have to be Mr. Jordan.

You forgot, remember on the graduation day? What name did you find out?

Noo way.

How can I forget his name?

Don't mind babes. After all he's so hot, even today he's looking like a true greek god and don't forget he's the topmost hottest and sexiest billionaire.. The Eros Jordan.

Shut up.

I don't need your mockery now.

Okay, but he really looks hot and sexy.

"God, please make mother earth open up and let her swallow me." I said to myself. Totally flushed in embarrassment.

Why he?

Why Mr. Rude?

God, What do you want from me?

Another one completed...

So what you guys think... what'll happen next...

Wanna know...

Then

....

Keep on reading

Love you all guys

Chapter 8

This chapter is dedicated to

Thanks for all your comments.

Eros's attire's pic for meeting Scarlett above...

Enjoy

Eros's POV

It's been two days when I said yes to meet that unknown girl.

Scarlett.

Yeah, same.

After that night my mom didn't even disturbed me nor even said anything.

I think she felt pity on you and forgot about the proposal.

I hope you're right.

I was in my office sitting on my chair and checking about the new deal that I signed yesterday.

It wasn't very tough deal to crack so it was very easy for me to grab the deal.

It's been a while since I met that bumping girl. Something is in her that everytime I see her I just get lost in an unknown feel.

I want to meet her again. There is something in her which attracts me towards her more and more. I wish I meet her again but without bumping.

I chuckled.

Hey lover boy, you should not be thinking of any other girl when your mom is booking you for another girl

My inner voice teased.

My train of thoughts got interrupted when my office doors bursted open and my mom came in with a huge smile.

And here comes the devil.

"How is my lovely son feeling today?" she cheerfully asked.

Isn't she so cheery today?

She's always cheerful.

"I'm good mom. How are you?" I said while getting up from my chair.

I walked towards my mom and she gave me a tight bone crushing hug.

Are your bones alright?

"I'm absolutely fine honey" she showed her toothy smile.

She proved that she had brushed her teeth.

Shut up.

"Want some water or anything?" I asked my mom out of courtesy as I took a glass of water for me.

"No dear" she smiled.

Isn't is she smiling a lot?

"Why so happy mom?" I asked as I took a sip of water.

"Why won't I be happy as my son would be meeting her soon to be wife tomorrow" she squealed by clapping her hands.

I choked on my water.

And here's the bomb strucked directly in your throat.

I was coughing badly when my mom started rubbing my back.

"Honey, are you alright?" She worriedly asked.

When I came back to my senses I said " yes mom" I cleared my throat "Don't call her my wife, she's not my wife." I warned.

"Yet." she cut me off.

"She'll soon tie knots with you and will become your lawful wife" she stated.

And here I was thinking that your mom felt pity on you and cancelled that proposal.

"As I was saying, you are meeting her tomorrow at The Chelsea's.All the bookings are done and your butt should be there at 12 noon, otherwise...." she evilly smiled.

No.. no. Say yes. Say Y E S.

"Do you wanna see my otherwise honey?" She dangerously asked.

Bro don't test her she is dangerous. I'm afraid of this side of hers.

"Oo-okay mom" I gulped.

I cleared my throat.

"I'll be there" I nervously smiled.

"Aww my lovely son. I know you won't say no to me" she grinned.

Pheww, you saved me from seeing a true devil.

And with that she left my office.

I hope everything happens fine tomorrow.

I also wish the same.

I took a deep breath and ignored all the negative thoughts and concentrated on my work.

----****-----

(Next morning....)

I woke up on the beeping noise of my clock.

I opened my eyes, it's 7:00 AM. I shutted the alarm off and went to bathroom to do my morning rituals.

Then after coming out of the room I wore my sweatpants and a Tee and went for jogging.

After coming back from jogging I went to my room to take a nice hot shower. After the shower I dried myself and wore my fresh sweatpants and take a look at the time, 9:30. I have a lot of time, with that I went to the kitchen to have my breakfast.

I'm not going to the office till that meeting with the unknown girl.

Scarlett, her name is Scarlett.

Oh, you are up. Good morning. Did you sleep well?

Nope, your mom's dangerous face was coming into my view but thanks for asking.

I rolled my eyes.

Suddenly my phone started ringing and my mom's name showed up on the screen.

Speak of devil and the devil appears. All the very best.

Oh, hush up.

I received her call within time."Good morning mom" I greeted.

"Oh, good morning dear. I can see you are up" she said.

"Yeah mom" I briefly said by taking a bite of my toast.

"So, you remember no? That you are meeting Scarlett today at 12?" She asked.

"Yes mom, I remember" I replied.

"That's good. So are you ready?" She questioned.

"Mom, I have to meet her at 12. So why hurry?" I said.

"Son its quarter past 10 and you should start getting ready. I dont want you to be late. Now hurry up" she stated.

I sighed.

"Okay mom I'll get ready. Bye mom" I said.

"Okay son, enjoy. Love you. Bye" with that she hung up the phone.

Your mom is pure evil.

First time in my life I wanna agree with you.

I left the kitchen and walked towards my closet. What should I wear today?

I took out a black jeans and white shirt and a black blazer.

After getting ready I took a glimpse of time.

Holy shit.

Its 11:30. I'm going to be late.

Run bro run, otherwise your mom will have you in dinner.

Yeah.

I exited my home and went to parking and uncovered my ferrari. Today I'll drive by myself. I got seated and drove to my destination.

When I reached The Chelsea's, I parked my ferrari in the parking. As I exited my car I can feel stares of the people.

When I turned around girls are looking at my side.

I smirked.

And continued to enter the restaurant.

When I entered I went to reception and asked for the bookings.

Suddenly a girl came and asked for the bookings under Mrs. Miller.

Her voice is so melodious so similar.

Similar?

Similar?

I was about to turn but I bumped into her. What the hell is with these girls and bumping?

"Sorry, It was my mistake..." when she looked up. She was not any girl, she was,

Scarlett.

With her sparkling blue eyes.

Did she planned or is she really loves to bump in every guy she see but now the main thing is..

What is she doing here?

I was unable to move my gaze from her. She was looking soo damn alluring in her white dress which is perfectly fitted on her curves. She's looking as beautiful as an angel.

Close your mouth otherwise flies will come in.

I closed my mouth.

She was accussing me for I don't know what. But she's looking hot, all worked up.

Lover boy, time to come out from the dream world. I'll give you your favourite candy.

Shut up.

I crossed my arms over my chest and glanced her from up to down.

She is indeed beautiful.

Yeah, with perfect curves and this dress suits her a lot.

Hey stop. You are shamelessly checking her out. She'll think she can control you with her looks.

Busted.

I controlled my feelings and composed myself.

She uncomfortably shifted.

She pointed her index finger at me.

"You..." she was about to say something but was cut off by a waiter.

"Mr. Jordan come with me. I'll show you your table" the waiter said to me.

I nodded. As I was about to move.

"Mam is there any chance that you are Scarlett Miller?" waiter asked.

She nodded.

"A table for both of you has been booked by Mrs. Miller, so come this way" the waiter said.

Whhhhhhaaaaaatttt??

Seriously or am I dreaming? She is the girl whom your mom selected for you to marry? Who keeps on bumping on you whenever she meet you. I'm starting to think that she has some kind of bumping disease.I can't believe this. Earth is really round.My trust on the world ended today.

She is the one whom my mom selected for me.

And she is none other than the.

Bumping girl.

Scarlett

Another one completed...

So what you guys think...

Whats going to happen next..

To know...

Then you have to

Keep on reading

Love you all guys a lot

21/03/2018

Chapter 9

Scarlett's POV

"A table for both of you has been booked by Mrs. Miller, so come this way" the waiter said.

I looked at him and he was looking at me.

For a few minutes we were staring each other.

Such a cliche moment.

Back to Earth Ms. Miller

He cleared his throat.

"First let's get seated Ms. Miller" he awkwardly said.

I nodded.

We followed the waiter's direction.

Soon we were seated on a private table. I can feel that the waiter is extra polite towards me.

"What would you both like to order?" the waiter asked, by looking only at me and ignoring Mr. Jordan.

At least someone is finding you beautiful.

Shush.

"Um..cappuccino for me with a blueberry muffin please" I said with an uncomfortable smile.

He also gave me his creepy smile. I shuddered at his smile. He wrote the order down and asked Mr. Jordan without even looking at his side.

I started feeling uncomfortable under his gaze.

"One black coffee for me with a cheesecake and can you stop eye raping my date, and tell me what is your name? I want to have a talk with your manager." Mr. Jordan huffed.

Aww, your knight in shining armor.

But calm him down otherwise he'll soon be puffing out the smoke from his ears.

"It's okay Mr. Jordan" I tried to calm him down.

He looked at me and nodded.

Oh.. thank god he stopped. I thought he'll turn this restaurant into a battle field.

"S-sorry Sir" the waiter apologized.

The waiter's face was priceless. Bravo Eros.

"Now leave and bring us our order." Mr. Jordan ordered.

The waiter hurriedly left from there.

"Thank you, Mr. Jordan" I smiled at him.

"Eros is fine. Mr. Jordan makes me feel old and no problem, after all he ignored me." He said.

Huh?

Seriously?

He did all this because that waiter guy ignored him.

Seriously he is Mr. Rude.

Exactly that's what I'm saying.

I raised an eyebrow at him. He winked at me.

I rolled my eyes.

He is so damn rude and self obsessed, you can't marry him. Say no to him and say bye to him for ever.

"Okay, Mr. uh.. I mean Eros" I nervously said.

"So Ms. Miller" Eros said.

"You can call me Scarlett" I told him.

There was an awkward silence between us.

Say something.

What should I say?

I don't know? Just say anything.Say that he's sexy, no not that say that he's too sexy for you.

What?

Umm, nothing. Forget it. Firstly eat the food then say bye to him.

Food is much more important.

True.

Soon the orders came but with different waiter and he didn't looked at me like the previous one. After serving he left.

"So Scarlett, how are you?" He said after taking a sip from his coffee to broke the silence.

Why is he being so polite now? After all he can't think anything else except him.

I took a sip of my coffee and took a deep breath.

Here we go.

It's now or never.

"Cut the crap and stop being someone you're not " I started.

"What?" His eyes widens.

"We both know that our moms planned all this and we both don't want it. We don't wanna marry each other, so it's better we both end it right here. Why marry when we don't even know each other, let's stop our mom's stupidity." I stated bluntly.

He gave me a confused look by frowning.

"Listen, we don't even know each other, so why don't we end all this drama" I said.

"What do you mean? Ms.. uh.. Scarlett" he confusingly asked.

"You don't wanna marry me I don't wanna marry you, feelings are mutual. So you tell my mom that you don't like me and I'll tell your mom that I don't like you. End of discussion." I stated while taking a sip of my coffee.

He frowned.

"And why do you think I would do that?" He asked.

"Simple, we are not made for each other. You love only yourself and I can't marry someone who thinks all of himself and we don't even know anything about each other besides our names. So this relationship is not gonna workout. Why not end it now" I coolly said.

He was getting annoyed as I was speaking

"So? What fantastic idea do you have, Scarlett?" He scoffed.

"You'll call my mom and tell her that you don't like me and I'm not compatible for you, etc etc etc. and I'll do the same with your mom" I said.

"What's the surety that our mom will not try to bind us again?" He questioned.

"We both will say a lot of crap about each other, like you can say that I'm not fit for you. I'm bitchy or a gold digger or I'm ugly, whatever you wish and I'll do the same for you with my mom"I told him.

He put his finger under his chin as he was thinking.

He's looking so cute doing that, what a mesmerizing view.

You are right.

I put my elbow on the table then put my face in my palm and took the opportunity to watch the beautiful view in front of me.

Brown hairs, green eyes, perfectly sculpted jawline, pink plump limps, little beard doing justice on his look. He's looking so sexy in his blazer and white crisp shirt. I can see he's having abs. I wanna touch them.

My train of thoughts got interrupted when someone cleared his throat.

Oh my neighbor's shit! you were drooling over him.

"Liked what you see?" he teased.

Busted.

I shifted embarrassingly and ignored him.

"Uh.. I think I should go now. Nice meeting you Mr. Jordan, hope you'll find you perfect match soon" I said getting up.

I was about to shake hands with him but he hugged me.

What the heck?

Mmm... his cologne, so amazing so delicious.

Scarlett Miller control yourself.

I abruptly pushed him and nodded my head and I quickly walked out from there.

What the hell happened in there?

What was I even doing?

I took a deep breath to calm my beating heart.

Forget it, you should be happy that the problem is sorted and now you can do whatever you want.

I grinned.

Yeaaahhhh.

I started doing my happy dance but soon felt people's stare at me.

Control babes control.

I flushed. I quickly took a taxi and went from there putting my head down in embarrassment.

What is happening to me today?

After half an hour when I reached my home I paid the driver and went towards my home.

I stood at entrance for sometime and planned every thing that I should say to my mom.

He would have called your mom by now and she might know everything.

I took a deep breath and entered my home. I see my mom she ran towards me and hugged me in a bone crushing hug.

I'll pray for your bones. I can feel the sadness.

"Thank you, Thank you, Thank you so much honey. You made me proud. I know you'll never fail me. I love you my baby" she said while showering kisses allover my face.

What? What is she saying? Have your mom gone mad because of the rejection?

I can see tears in her eyes.

What happened? Why is she crying?

How would I know?

Then ask her stupid.

"What happened mom? Why are you so crying? And why do you sound so happy?" I confusingly asked.

"These are the tears of happiness my baby and you don't know? May be he wants to surprise you? " she mumbled the last part to herself.

He?

"Who mom?" I asked.

"Your would be husband, Eros Jordan" she said in a duh tone.

"This time I remembered my son-in-law's name" she chirpily said.

My eyes widen.

What? Am I missing something here?

Not only you. I'm also missing something.

"What about him mom?" I curtly asked.

"Don't be rude, he's your future husband, be polite towards him" my mom said.

Now I'm getting annoyed.

"Mom? Please tell me what about him?" I annoyingly asked.

"He called me a few minutes ago and told me about your meeting and..." she said.

I think I can't hear it.

My heartbeats were on full speed.

Something's going to happen that you won't like.

Oh shut up. Let my mum complete her sentence.

Don't tell me that I didn't warned you.

I wont.

Sure?

Shut up.

No one loves me.

I groaned.

"He said he liked you and your behaviour and found you beautiful and at-tractive. He said he'll be glad to marry you" she said cheerfully by clapping her hands.

I froze on my spot,

My eyes widen.

Whaaatttt? Am I listening things or she said he'll marry you?

Pffft, She's a real good actor. I actually believed her. She's so funny.

"Mom you're lying no? You're joking, right?" I nervously asked.

"Why would I lie? He called me and told me all this" she innocently said.

This is a whole lot of shit. I can't handle anymore. I'm fainting.

Oh God, why is all this happening this to me?

Why didn't he say no?

He betrayed me.

I'm not going to leave him.He'll know, he messed with the wrong person.

That's the spirit my soldier.

Tell him who you are and what you can do.

Eros Jordan, I'll kill you.

Another one done

Sooo...What do you guys think....Why did Eros said yess to her....What's in his mind...To know...

Keep on reading...

Please do comment me your views..

Love you all loads...

22/03/2018

Chapter 10

Eros's POV

"A table for both of you has been booked by Mrs. Miller, so come this way" the waiter said.

I was in a shock that she is the one my mom selected for me.

An unknown feel of happiness erupted inside me that she's the one.

Bro you are getting crazy day by day. I thought I was insane but noo, you proved me that I'm your inner voice.

I shaked my head and ignored all my inner voices.

And cleared my throat.

"First let's get seated Ms. Miller" I awkwardly said.

She nodded.

She started walking and I walked behind her.

Damn she looks beautiful from back also.

Right. Oh stop, why am I listening to you?

Because I'm awesome.

I rolled my eyes.

Soon we were seated on a private table.

The waiter is showing more attention towards her.

I'm not liking it. How can he look at her in that way?

Take a chill pill man.

Soon the waiter came and he took order from us while staring Scarlett. How can he look at her like that.

A sudden rush of anger flew through me. I clenched my fists.

I took a deep breath as I don't wanna create a scene in front of her.

He's not only staring at Scarlett but he was eye raping her.

I can see she's getting uncomfortable under his gaze. She was shifting in her seat.

No one else can see her in that way.

Only you can?

Yeah.

What?

Nothing.

He also gave his toothy smile to her.

Oh how fun it would be in breaking his teeth. Then his smile would be priceless.

He wrote the order down and asked me without even glancing at me.

Seriously? Can't he see me.

Calm down. Scarlett's gonna get scared by your flared nostrils.

But he exceeded the limit, now no more. I'll tell him what happens when he sees someone, who is mine.

Your's?

Yes. Mine.

She's not your's.

Yet.

I ignored my inner voice after that.

I'll show him where does he stands, bloody creep.

I scolded him for looking at my date like that and making her uncomfortable. I'm going to have a talk with the manager after the date.

Wow man, getting possesive huh? nice, but sometimes act possesive for me too, please.

Now you are irritating me.

Oh sorry. I'm not here. Please continue with your battle.

I calmed only when I heard a melodious voice, when I looked at the source of voice, ohh, so Scarlett is theone with the melodious voice.

Her words calmed my nerves down. Strange. I sighed and nodded my head towards her.

Amazing, you calmed down by just listening her words and here I was literally begging you to calm down and you ignored me. I hate you.

I once again ignored my voices.

I told her that I did all that things because I don't want her to feel that I felt possesive over her. It will harm my reputation.

Yup, you are Eros Jordan, every girl wants you. You can't show her that you were jealous over her.

Hey, I was not jealous.

Yes, you were.

No, I was not.

Yes, you were.

No, I was not.

Yes.

Noo.

Yes.

Oh shut up. Let me concentrate here.

When I looked at her she was busy in thinking something and a frown was on her face.

She looked cute.

Control you emotions man.

After few minutes she opened her mouth and started telling me her marvellous or more like stupid plan to make me say no to her and to tell our moms that we don't wanna marry each other.

She really don't wanna marry you.

As if I'm going to follow her orders. I'll do whatever I wish.

And you very well know you can't do that whatever she's saying? You know your mom is a pure devil and she'll not leave you. She'll eat you raw. Man don't listen to her. She don't know your mom.

I was busy in my own thoughts but when I looked at herShe was drooling over me.

I smirked.

I know your charms man.

I cleared my throat to gain her attention.

"Liked what you see" I teased.

Caught red handed.

She blanched.

And suddenly got up from her seat to leave.

She didn't even wait for your reply. She just ordered you.

She was about to shake hands with me instead I hugged her.

Amazing, she's totally amazing. My mom was right. She's perfect for me. Her fragrance, fully toxic. I want to smell it daily. Her body was so soft against me. I want to feel her in my arms.

She abruptly pushed me and with a nod she quickly walked out from left me standing.

What did I just do?

Man you are whipped.

Hush up. Now what should I do.

Do you want to marry her?

May be or may be not. I'm not sure but I agreed to her, but she's different. I really want to know her more. But I can't betray her. What should I do now.

But when did you agree? She was the one who was saying everything and didn't even wait for you to respond.

True. I didn't accepted her proposal. A smile formed on my face.

Now let's make her mine.

I grinned.

Now call her mom and say yes to her.

Right. Let me take her mother's number from my mom.

When I got the number and instantly called her.

She received within two rings.

All the best man.

"Hello? Am I talking to Mrs. Miller" I asked.

"Speaking, who are you?" She asked.

"My name is Eros Jordan, son of your best friend Carol. The one whom your daughter met today" I told her.

"Oh, yes, yes, honey. How are you? And how was your meeting and how do you feel about my daughter?" She bombarded me with so many questions.

"I'm good and the meeting was good and I called you to inform you that"

I took a deep breath and spoke

"I find your daughter very interesting and very beautiful, I liked her a lot especially her behaviour and I'm ready to get married to her" I finally told her.

She squealed in my ear.

Damn! I'm sure that you are deaf by now.

"Thank you, Thank you so much son. I'm glad you liked my daughter. May God bless you" she cheerfully said.

"My pleasure, Mrs. Miller" I responded.

"I gotta go now, will talk to you later" with that I hung up the call.

Congrats bro, you finally found the one.

She will not sit quietly, she'll soon come to me to kill me. As soon as she'll know all the things.

Yeah, she's a fiesty one. Let's wait what will she do.

I chuckled to myself and soon left the restaurant and started driving towards my office.

Sacrlett you'll soon be mine.

Only mine.

Finally chapter completed...

Pheww

Hope you all like it..

Do vote and comment...

Love you all

23/03/2018

Chapter 11

- -

S carlett's POV

He, he is such a jerk, arrogant, creep, psycho, liar. Uhh.. How can he do this to me? He said no to me in the starting, so why in the hell he did this and said yes to my mom?

Ugh. I just hate him.

Go meet him and tell him who is he messing with. Go my one lady army. Tell him who Scarlett Miller is.

Don't he know me?

Just go. It's not the time for your stupidity.

I have to meet him. How could he betray me? That bloody stupid conceited idiot, Mr. Rude.

I won't leave you. You'll get to know who am I.

Go babes go. If you want any help just tell me.

We'll throw him from the topmost floor of his office building.

Or we can throw flower pots on his face, no, not on his face. He has a nice face but on his head yeah on his head, right?

May be he'll get some brain into his skull.

Or we can shoot him with a bazooka?

Last one is perfect, its my personal favourite.

Oh shut up. I don't need your idea now.

But I just wanted to help.

My inner voice whined.

I took my car out and entered his company address in the gps, and I drove to his office.

When I reached his office I asked the receptionist about his room. She told me it's at the topmost floor but I'm not allowed without an appointment. Like hell I'm not allowed.

As if we care. We will burn this office. Babe, do you have a matchstick.

Hush up.

Oh sorry, how can you have a matchstick, stupid me.

Exactly.

So you must have a lighter no?

I groaned.

Got it. I'll keep quiet and will enjoy the show.

From nowhere a guard came and he tried to grab me but I dodged him.

Hah, you're late.

I quickly entered the elevators and pressed the topmost floor number. I can still listen the yelling of the receptionist and the guard.

I exited the elevators and there stood a lady in her office attire. I asked her where is his office. She told me I can't go in because I don't have an appointment.

Appointment my ass.

I quickly ran from there and I barged into his room and saw him.

He was sitting on his chair. When I entered he looked up and soon the stupid lady came behind me.

"I didn't expect to get a visit from you so soon" he smirked.

He still have the audacity to smirk at you.

Don't worry I'll wipe that smirk soon.

I'll tell you buddy, how lucky you are going to be to get a visit from me.

"Sir, s-sorry sir. I told her not to enter but she didn't listened to anyone. Do you want me to call the security?" the lady asked hesitantly while shooting daggers at me.

Go to hell. Like your stupid security whom I just dodged will take me out.

"No. You can go. I'll take it from here" he dismissed her without even looking at her.

What the hell? He didn't even got up from his chair.

Mr. Rude.

She left the room closing the door after her.

"So, scar..."he started but I cut him off.

"It's Ms. Miller for you and how dare you? What the hell do you think of yourself, huh? You'll do whatever you want. Who gave you this right? You bloody sick arrogant rude jerk. How can you lie to me? You betrayed me. You creep, how could you, first you accepted my proposal and now you called my mum saying that you want to marry me, bullshit. I thought you were a nice guy but no, you are anything but nice. God.. why did I even listened to you in the first place" I said all in a single breath.

He was looking at me in astonishment, but didn't say anything so I continued.

"I thought you were also forced from your mother. I thought that I'll help you and me both but no, how can you take my or anyone's help. Taking help is out of your league. After all you are Mr. Rude, you are just, uh... " when I looked at him he was smiling a genuine smile, not a smirk but an actual smile.

"Mr.Rude, huh?" He said by taking steps towards me.

I audibly gulped. Shit! I rambled the name that I gave him infront of him.

Can't I keep my mouth shut? Why am I so stupid?

It is yet to be discovered.

He came close to me and trapped me between him and wall.

"When did I said yes to you?" he questioned.

I was about to reply but then I remembered, he never said yes.

I stood there in shock.

Yes, he didn't said yes to you. You just imposed him with all your bullshit without even giving him a chance to speak. So that he can share his views about your fantastic plan.

Damn! And you are telling me all this now.

I cleared my throat.

"You could have told me but you didnt, it's all your fault. You should have stopped me and told me about your views. I don't wanna marry you and I won't marry you, ever" I stated while shooting daggers at him.

Well done. Now he must be knowing that to whom he messed.

He was about to say something but I just pushed him with all the strength I got. He stumbled back because I caught him off guard.

"You are the one who started all this and you'll also be the one who'll stop all this bullshit. I don't care how, just do it and end this stupid drama" I said.

And was about to leave but stopped and turned around and said "I hope this is our last meet. I wish we don't meet each other again. Have a nice life ahead Mr. Eros Jordan." I curtly said and left his office.

I held my chin high while walking out of the office.

On my way to exit I met the familiar annoyed faces of the receptionist but I ignored them and went towards my car and drove back home.

When I reached home my mom was nowhere to be seen. I tried to call her but no response, so I just walked toward my room.

I change my clothes into a pink shorts and white tank top and hair in a messy bun.

Ah! home sweet home. I'm gonna rest now, every thing is sorted now. That handsome and sexy billionaire is out of our way.

Yeah, but don't forget the handsome and sexy billionaire is also Mr. Rude. Now I can live peacefully.

Babe? Why did he said yes to your mom? I think his mom also forced him to do so, but why didn't he grabbed the opportunity?

You know I was also thinking the same and why me? He can get any girl he want. Why is he persistent towards marrying me? I'm not that hot and sexy, like the girls he had dated.

May be he likes you.

Hey, he's Mr. Rude. He don't do that love things and I don't think he will ever love me. May be he's taking some kind of revenge on me? Because of my stupid bumping.

Any thing can be possible. Now rest and let me also rest. I need my beauty sleep. I need to look good.

Yaa, yaa, you should look good and who is going to see you?

You hurt me. You are also becoming just like him.

Suddenly loud sound of knocking on the door heard.

Who can be at the door at this time?

Whosoever is knocking that loud, would have to pay for disturbing my beauty sleep.

May be, my mom came.

But she has her own set of keys.

Yeah right. Let's check then.

I climbed down the stairs.

The knocking is getting louder by every second.

"Coming" I yelled.

The person who's knocking is so restless.

I walked towards the main door open it.

I froze on my spot.

Bundles of shit.

The person standing there was none other than,

Eros.

He was standing there.

When he looked at me he kept on staring me from up to down with an unknown expression.

What is it with him? Why did he came here? What does he want?Is this his way to take revenge?

I'm really getting scared this time.

"Well hello Scarlett... baby" he said with wink.

Why did he came?

What does he want?

Oh God.

Another chapter done...

Phewww

So... what do you think will happen next...

To wanna know...

Keep on reading...

Please do vote and comment for my story...

Love you guys

23/03/2018

Chapter 12

E ros's POV

I was sitting in my office, happy that Scarlett would be mine soon.

Yeah, she would be yours. Please don't forget me.

I can't even if I want to.

Hey, I think we forgot something. something very important.

What?

Don't know, can't point it out.

Okay, when you remember do tell me.

Then I buried myself in my work.

Oh damn!

I remember.

What?

That we are forgetting something.

And what is that?

You forget to tell the devil I mean your mom about the meeting. She'll kill you man.

Shit, you're right I should call her.

I took my phone and dialed my mom's number.

"Hey mom" I said.

"Oh, you got time to remember me, so nice of you" she taunted.

Apologise to her now, otherwise she'll kick your butt.

"Um... sorry mom, I got indulged in work that's why I forgot to call you" I apologised.

"Forget it, now tell me how was your meeting with Scarlett?" She excitingly asked.

I smiled.

Man you are whipped.

I shaked my head to remove all the thoughts.

"Yes mom, it was nice meeting her and I liked her and decided that I'll marry her. I found her quite interesting " I stated.

She squealed in my ears through the phone.

Your ears man, helllooooo, heelllllloooo, can you listen to me?

Shut up.

Oh you can.

"I'm so happy son. I love you so much. I know she's right for you. I'm glad that you liked her" she said.

I think she must be jumping right now because of happiness.

I chuckled.

"Have you told her mom about it? Oh my god, we have a lot of things to do, your engagement, your wedding, your honeymoon" she rambled.

Whoa! I think she also planned the names for your children, she is super-fast.

"Relax mom. I just said yes today, all things will be managed, don't panic" I calmed her.

She took a deep breath.

"Your right son. I'm so much happy because of you." she said while taking a deep breath to calm herself.

"I'm glad that you are happy" I said.

"Okay son. I got to go now. I should congratulate my dear friend too. Love you son, Bye" she said after that she hung up.

Your mom is not that bad, may be, I was wrong about her.

Traitor.

Hush.

I heard sounds of people speaking, especially yelling of Maya.

What's happening?

Let's wait and watch, because I also don't know.

I shrugged.

Suddenly my room's doors burst open and I know it very well who came making such a hurricane.

Right man,she's really a beautiful hurricane.

Hey she's mine.

And I'm your's too.

Unfortunately.

Rude.

I ignored him and said looking at her with a smirk "I didn't expected to get a visit from you so soon."

I know that she'll come but I seriously didn't expected so soon.

The sooner the better.

She was kind of taken back from my words, my smirk grew wider.

I'm enjoying it.

Me too, I said to my inner voice.

My thoughts were interrupted by Maya, my secretary, when she told me that Scarlett entered without any appointment.

After I told Maya that I can handle from here, she left the room closing the door after her.

Let's know, why did she barged in like that? Bro, she must have dodged all your security to come here, she's professional.

After a few minutes of bickering I came to know about that stupid name that she chose for me.

Mr. Rude.

I can't control my laugh at her chosen name.

Nice name,

I want to laugh but I can't. I have to stop my emotions. I put my serious look on.

And started taking slow steps towards her.

As I get closer to her I can notice her body stiffen.

Man, she's getting effected by you.

I can see she is getting nervous.

I don't know why but I felt proud that I have this effect on her.

I came closer to her and trapped her between me and the wall.

She looks even more prettier from a close up view.

Sparkling blue eyes, brown hairs coming on her face her cheeks turning pink. Her long cute eyelashes.

My hands were itching to touch her.

She looks so cute when she is mute but when she started talking.. Uhh!

She started shouting that I betrayed her I didn't say yes when she told me say yes, that we had deal etc.

After I told her that I never accepted her offer to not to marry her, she blanched.

Her little eyes widen. Like she has seen a ghost.

After few minutes of silence

She came back on that track that I have to say no to her mom that I will not marry her.

And once again without listening to me, she told me to reject her and left storming out of my office.

Without even listening to my god damn reply!

Either she's naive or she's actually stupid.

I think the latter one is right.

After she left I was standing there for don't know how much time.

This is the first. No girl have refused me but she. Why is she so persistent to not to marry me. She'll be the death of me. She's a unique, totally crazy, always do whatever comes to her mind, so full of life.

She doesn't know, who am I .I will not let her go so easily. I want her to be mine.

After knowing that she's the girl who my mum selected for me an unknown kind of feeling ran throughout my body like I have to make her mine a kind of possessiveness for her which I never felt for anyone.

I won't let you leave me Scarlett I haven't even tried to impress you yet, and I know this is my only chance.

I am coming to you my dear Scarlett.

She thinks that she won't marry me, but I'll make sure that she'll marry me, only me, no one else. She'll only be mine.

My Scarlett.

I smiled.

Uhh, you are scaring me man. What are you going to do?

Just wait and watch.

I exited my office room and told Maya to cancel all my appointments. I'm going somewhere.

While exiting the building I called my mom and asked Scarlett's address. Let's show her a trailer of me.

Ooooo, I'm liking it. I wanna see, what do you have in your mind?

I headed towards my car and entered the address in gps and drove towards Scarlett's house.

I'm coming Scarlett baby to let you know you're Mine.

I reached in front of her house. I exited my car and head towards the main door.

I took a deep breath and started knocking the door.

After a few minutes a figure came into my view.

The figure was wearing pink shorts and white tank top and when my gaze come up towards the face.

My Scarlett was standing there in shock looking so hot yet innocent in that outfit.

She's looking beautiful plus cute plus hot in those clothes. Her long sexy legs, her curvy figure, she looks sexy.

She was looking at me in pure shock.

She didn't expected me at all, amazing.

I smirked at her.

She was dumbfounded by my sudden visit.

"Well hello Scarlett... baby" I said with wink.

Great job man. I'm proud of you.

Let's tell her to whom she belongs.

Her expressions were totally priceless.

What do you think of the chapter??

Do you guys liked it??

Do tell me..

Thank you so much for reading.

Why did Eros came to Scarlett's home?

Wanna know?

Then...

Wait for my next update

Love you guys

Keep on voting and commenting.

24/03/2018

Chapter 13

S carlett's POV

What is he doing here??

I asked this question around ten times to myself.

Then stupid, raise your voice and ask him. Then only you are going to know.

You are right. I should ask him why is he here.

By the way he's looking so hot in his tired look. His hairs were disheveled, perfectly lying on his forehead, wow. He's the true definition of handsome. When did you get so lucky?

Oh shush. Don't distract me, let me know why is he here.

I put my both hands on my hips and asked him angrily.

"What the hell are you doing here? Is there any problem with you? Can't you understand my words? Are you deaf? Let me repeat once again for you, I said I . Don't . Want . Any . Connection . With . You. Am I made myself clear now? Why can't you just leave me alone?"I huffed furiously. Why the hell he can't understand?

First calm down, may be he came to apologise, listen to him.

He was looking at me in amazement with an annoying smirk. Ugghh.

What does he think, are you a joker? I don't mind but he can't say that to you directly.

You're the one who called me joker, how dare you?

Umm, um, I was... aa..

Shut up.

I concentrated on Eros again.

He was about to reply but my mom came from nowhere and interrupted him.

She was at home? In which corner was she hiding?

"Honey, is everything alright?? Who's at the door? And why are you not inviting him in?" My mom questioned.

I groaned.

"Um.. mom he is Mr. Eros Jordan, as you know" but I was cut of by the stupid Mr. Rude.

He came forward and put his hand in front of my mum to shake hands but instead, my mom crushed him in a tight hug.

Poor guy.

"Oh, Mr. Jordan. How are you? Is everything alright? Why did you came at this hour?" Mom questioned worryingly.

He smiled at my mom and was about to say something but this time I interrupted him.

"Ah mom, he's about to go" I said while fluttering my eyelashes.

You won't let him speak no?

Nope.

He turned towards me and said "Oh Scarlett, why are you so persistent in making me go. You very well know I came here to meet you"

I choked on my saliva. I coughed loudly.

My mum looked or we can say glared at me.

"Is he right Scarlett? Why are you not letting him to talk to you. Poor guy came all the way to talk to you and you're not talking to him. That's very bad Scarlett" my mum said.

I'm sure I saw Eros smirking his victorious smirk but he quickly replaced it with poor guy's look.

Devil disguised as a hot hunk.

Cruel world.

"Aa.. mom.. actually he-" I was cut off by Eros.

"You know what Mrs. Miller, I think I should go. I'll come some another time. I don't think Scarlett wants to talk to me" he pouted.

Seriously?

Please mom don't stop him. Please make him leave.

But what does he want to talk?

Bazooka's idea is still in list if you want.

I ignored my stupid voices.

"No, you can talk to her as much as you want. You both are soon getting married. You can come whenever you want. She will take you to her room, right Scarlett?" my mum said while staring at me with narrowed eyes, like daring me to say no to her.

A shiver ran through my body.

Don't say no if you want to live.

I turned towards him and see him smirking.

I want to wipe that stupid smirk off his face.

"This way please" I said with a grim look and showed him the way to my room.

He nodded and followed me not forgetting to say thank you to my mum.

I walked towards my room and he was behind me.

Once I entered he locked the door behind him.

What?

Why did he locked the door?

If he's trying to scare me, no more.

That's the spirit. I pushed my inner voice.

I'm already scared, you win Eros.

I rolled my eyes.

Seriously?

Without even trying?

Eros turned towards me and took dangerous but slow step towards me and said "Scarlett baby, you have a very bad habit of not listening to others point of views. You directly jump on to the conclusions and that's why I have to come here. That's really bad of you. But, nevermind"

Whaaaatttt?

Scarlett baby?

Conclusions?

What is he talking about?

He came more closer to me and slided a hand on my waist.

My breath hitched.

A different kind of spark ignited in my body. I haven't felt this feeling ever. What is he doing to me?

I was unable to move as his grip was so tight yet gentle on me, his closeness is making my mind go numb.

He stared me for a few minutes which I felt like hours,

In his arms, covered in his delicious fragrance, ummm..

Stop! Stop right there.

After a few minutes he continued, but with a serious tone.

"Scarlett, you will marry me, only me and no one else. You'll be mine Scarlett. You were mine from the moment I laid my eyes on you. You'll become my lawfully wedded wife and you won't disobey or say no to me at any cost" he stated.

What? He wants to marry you?

But for an unknown reason I was blushing. May be because of our close-ness. A shiver ran throughout my body,

I was not able to comprehend his words.

What is happening to me?

When I looked at him,

He was smirking at my condition.

He's looking hot.

Yeah, totally.

He glided the back of his fingers across my now red cheeks,

"You look adorable when you blush" he said in a husky voice.

I think I must have turned a few shades darker of red because of his comment.

"Before I was doing this for my mom but now, I'm doing this all for me. I want to become selfish for you. I want you in my life, I want to spend my life with you, grow old with you. I want you to be mine, be my wife, my Scarlett, only mine " he said with so much passion and determination while touching my cheek with his knuckles.

His touch was leaving unknown feeling. I want to drown myself in the foreign sensations which was making my body betray me. I can feel his minty and warm breath on my face, we were so close. His lips were few inches away from me. My heart is going to come out from my chest. His closeness was making my mind numb.

Why can't I move myself? My body is totally betraying me.

His cologne was filled in my nostrils, ummm.

Slowly slowly he moved his face further towards me and I don't know why I closed my eyes.

I felt something soft on my cheek, my eyes shot open. He pecked me. his lips linger for a few minutes.

Did he just kissed me, OMG.

My eyes and moth were wide open. Not knowing what to say.

He chuckled at my condition.

Rude.

I gathered myself up.

"And why would you think that I'll marry you?" I awkwardly asked, more like a whisper.

"Oh baby, you have to. You would say no to your mom, huh? You know that your single no can break the bond between my mom and your mom. Do you want that? Her only friend breaks all her bond with your mom? Will you become selfish and let their friendship break? I don't expect you to become that selfish and if your mom says no then I know a way to how to make her say yes" He asked while nuzzling his nose on my neck and inhaling my scent.

His touch is making it hard for me to think. But I can't let this friendship break. My mom will totally break. After dad, Carol was the one who was with her. She supported her. I know she is like her sister. I can't break the bond. I can't be selfish and let her loose her only friend.

What should I do now?

"My mom will come day after tomorrow to discuss all the preparations of the wedding, go with her and buy whatever you want" he said still touching my cheeks.

He's so confident. He knows I won't break my mom's bond with Carol.

Why is he so rude? Why can't he see that I don't wanna marry him?

He once again moved his face towards my neck, my eyes closes on its instant, oh no no, I can't handle it anymore, my knees were shaking, his grip was making me stand otherwise till now I would be on the floor.

He inhaled a deep breath in my hairs and kissed on my sweet spot. I stopped myself to moan.

Goosebumps rose all over my body.

Suddenly his face was moved away and my eyes were still closed. Trying to calm myself.

Is he gone?

I opened an eye and he was gone. He was not here anymore.

I released my breath.

Damn! What happened to me? Why didn't I pushed him away? My body was liking the closeness with him.

The famous Eros Jordan kissed you, oh my god. I can't believe it.

It's just a peck on cheek, nothing more.

Then why are you red?

Because I wanna compete with a tomato, Happy?

Very.

I ignored her and I hurriedly exited my room and saw him climbing down the stairs.

My mom came again from I don't know where.

Is you mum playing hide and seek with herself?

"Is everything okay with you both?" she asked.

Eros stopped on his place and turned towards me.

How does he know that I'm behind him?

Because you climb down the stairs like a baby elephant, who makes loud thumping noise.

Hush.

I turned my face away as I don't want him to see me in this condition.

But still I looked at him from the corner of my eye.

He smiled a genuine smile, not a smirk. He really smiled. Wow, he looked so cute and those dimples are the cherry on the cake.

I blushed again.

"Yes, everything's good and Mrs. Miller we both want to tell you something. We both decided to get married by the end of the week and in two days we'll have our engagement ceremony" he smiled his toothy smile.

I was dumbstruck standing there, not able to move my body.

What did he just said?

Oh no, no, please let it be a dream. Please.

It's not. He's marrying you within a week.

Oh god.

I can't have anymore. I'm fainting.

"Yes! I'm so happy. You both are getting married. You'll be my son-in-law. I'm finally going to see my little Scar getting married. I'm going to be a grandmother soon" my mom squealed.

Grandmother?

Seriously?

Faster than Usain Bolt.

"But why so soon? How will we manage all preparations in one week?" My mom asked.

"Don't worry Mrs. Miller. I'll manage everything" he said with assurance.

She nodded.

"My mom will come tomorrow to discuss all the preparation of wedding" I told her.

She smiled.

"I think I should go now" he said glancing at his watch.

"Okay dear. Take care.Sweetheart, why don't you go with him, to see him off" my mom asked,which was more like an order, which I have to follow.

I nodded with a fake smile.

He was waiting for me and looking at me in astonishment.

As I came near him.

"What?" I questioned.

"Um, your cheeks are still red" He chuckled.

I touched my cheeks and once again that incident came to my mind.

I again blushed.

This time he laughed out loud.

"Don't you wanna go home?" I asked getting annoyed.

"I was thinking to go but if you want me to stay. I won't mind, wifey" he teased with a wink.

Wifey? Sounds cute.

I groaned"uhh...don't call me that"

"What?"he innocently asked.

"Whatever you just said in the end" I said.

"Oh..you don't wanna send me home. Aww honey" he again teased.

"Not that...uhh...the last word which you used" I huffed.

"I seriously don't know, Scar, why don't you tell me?" he smiled an innocent smile.

"I hate you" I said.

"I know you don't " he said with a wink and came close to me and kissed my cheek.

Once again, ladies and gentlemen, once again I turned red like a tomato.

I groaned.

He chuckled.

"Good night wifey" he winked.

He was about to go to his car but stopped on his stop and turned around and said looking at me up to down.

"By the way, you got sexy legs down there, Mrs. Jordan" he winked.

What the hell?

I tried to cover my legs, in response I heard his laughter.

His laugh is very cute.

What am I even saying?

What is happening to you?

He got seated in his car and soon drove off.

Seriously, what is happening with me?

Why he has to be the one?

Most importantly why he has to be so hot?

How will I manage my life with,

Mr. Rude.

Another chapter completed...

Hope you guys like it..

Do vote and comment...

Love y'all

26/03/2018

Chapter 14

Scarlett's today's attireAbove

Scarlett's POV

The very next morning I woke up early as no sleep came in the night.

I can still feel his touch, his smell, how close he was to me.

I groaned.

What is happening to me?

You are getting more stupid. Nothing else.

Don't forget you're my inner voice.

Unfortunately.

Shut up.

I have called my friends so that I can meet them. I wore a black top and white skinny jeans with black heels and with little make up and pink lip gloss, I was ready to go.

We were meeting at our favourite cafe, we usually hang out there. They have a very calm surroundings which will not be calm anymore when we'll reach there.

I reached there and searched for the familiar faces and soon found them, they were seated on a table near the window. I can tell from their faces that they are annoyed.

Surely they will be, you are late.

I hurriedly went there and got seated.

"Why are you late?" Sonya asked.

"You know I'm not a free guy. I have so many dates pending. I left them all waiting." Richie said teasingly.

"Umm.. sorry guys but I got engaged in something" I said without meeting their gaze.

"What happend?" Sonya asked.

I was not able to meet their gaze, so I put my head down.

"Look at us" they said.

When I meeted their gaze they got worried.

"What happened?" this time it was Richie.

Tell them, they'll surely help you out from this drama.

"Um, my mom arranged my marriage" I said.

"What?" Richie shocks.

I love my friends. Only they care for me.

"With whom? Is he hot and sexy?" Sonya asked.

Seriously Sonya?

I rolled my eyes.

When they'll know, they'll help you to leave him.

"Mm... Eros Jordan" I said.

They both froze on their spot, their eyes widen.

Exactly. Perfect, they are going right.

"Eros Jordan? Omg! The same guy you bumped, your mom is seriously amazing, can your mom adopt me please" Sonya excitedly said.

Huh?

"Wow. I didn't think he was an arranged marriage kind of guy. But he'll be superb for you. You both will look awesome together" Richie said.

"So when is the wedding?" They both asked getting happy.

Are they your real friends?

I narrowed my eyes at them.

"What?" They said in unison.

"You guys are happy, why?" I asked.

"Because our best friend is getting married to the most handsome and sexy ceo. I envy you for that but you're my friend I forgive you and most importantly we are going to do shopping, makeup, party and lots of food" Sonya cheerfully said.

I was shocked.

Richie continued "yeah, lots of food and some hot and sexy chicks. The ceo guy must have some beauties around her"

What the hell?

Seriously? What is it with Eros? Even his name make them his fan.

"You guys are seriously my friends no?" I questioned.

"Of course we are. That's why we are happy for you" Richie said.

"But I'm not happy. How can you both be happy? I want a marriage that have love in that, not an arrangement " I sadly said.

"Aww honey, you should be happy. He's a good guy and after Joel dumped me, arranged marriages are the best. Love can happen anytime with anyone and at the most unexpected time and with the most unexpected person" she told me while hugging me.

Yeah, Joel dumped her and within a week he was committed to another girl, Betty. She's such a dumb bimbo.

"Exactly, you should be happy. I never thought that someone is going to marry you" Richie teased.

I punched him on his shoulder. He shreaked.

I rolled my eyes and smiled at both of them and told them about what happened.

Suddenly my phone started ringing. I ignored it because it was an unknown number.

After few minutes it again ranged.

I excused myself and picked it up.

"Yes?" I questioned.

"Hey babe" the person asked. His voice was familiar, but who is he.

"Who are you?" I curtly asked. Sonya and Richie were looking at me to know who is at the call. I just shrugged.

"Don't tell me. You forgot me, that's really rude of you. I'm your future hot and sexy hubby, Eros Jordan." he teasingly said.

"How did you get my number? And what do you want?" I questioned him. Both my friends asked me about the person on the call. I mouthed Eros to them.

They both smirked and started to kissing actions.

Which made me to roll my eyes.

"I have my sources and I want only one thing... you" he stated.

My heart skipped a beat.

"Go to hell" I curtly said. Both my friends were grinning like idiots. I really want to smack them.

"Aww, honey don't be rude. I'm standing in front of the cafe in which you are in. Come and meet me. I don't like to wait. Come faster" he said more like an order.

"And why would I do that?" I asked by raising my eyebrow knowing that he can't see.

"You want me to come inside? Aww, you want to tell the whole world that you belong to me and soon you'll becoming Mrs. Jordan. How sweet of you. I'm coming in as you said " He said but I cut him in middle.

No way. He's a famous guy and he'll attract the people's attention and may be the paparazzi too.

You're right.

"Wait. I'm coming. You don't have to come inside" With that I hung up the call.

I told my friends that I have to go and will tell them what happened. They wished me all the best and to control my emotions and not to do something stupid.

What have I done to have friends like them?

I hurriedly exited the cafe, the most sexiest figure was standing there leaning on his car. He was in deep thoughts which makes him to look more sexy and the worst thing is girls were drooling over him.

What a mouth watering view.

An unknown feeling came over me and quickly walked towards him.

Possesive much, huh?

No, I'm not.

When he noticed me a smile came on his face which made him look ten times handsome. He came closer and inhaled in my hair and kissed my cheek.

My cheeks heated.

"Hello there, wifey" he said.

"Shut up, I'm not your wi- whatever" I huffed.

"You'll soon be" he winked.

I rolled my eyes.

He's right.

He opened the passenger door just like a gentleman. I got seated then he jogged to other side and got seated.

Aww, he's so sweet.

Traitor.

"Why are you here?" I asked by crossing my hands.

He smiled.

"Can't I meet my future wife?" he teased.

I groaned, in response he chuckled. We drove off to don't know where.

"Where are we going?" I asked.

He ignored me.

"Can't you tell me? Where are you taking me?" I again asked.

But no response.I groaned.

"Helllooooo? Eros? Can.. you...listen... to...me?"I yelled by doing actions with my hand.

He must be deaf by now from your constant yelling.

"Can't you keep calm and wait? Jeez, why do you speak so much? Now keep your mouth shut till we reach the destination, otherwise I have many interesting ways to shut your mouth. Wanna try?" He winked.

I averted my gaze from him and looked outside the window. We have crossed the city. I can see more trees were coming in my view.

Is he going to kidnap you? And then kill you?

"Are you going to kidnap me and keep me as a hostage and then you'll kill me in an deserted place?" I innocently asked.

"What? Why would you think that? Firstly you came with me with your wish and I don't have to kidnap you when you are soon going to be my wife and will be staying with me. And why would I kill you. I know you're annoying but I can't kill you" he winked.

He's right. He didn't kidnapped me because I came with my consent and about killing me, I know he wont. Then why isn't he telling me about where we are going? Uhh, I have to wait till we reach.

I groaned.

After sometime the car came to an halt. Eros exited the car and came to my side to open the door.

Finally.

I exited the car and looked at my surroundings.

I don't know where am I?

Then a cliff came into my view, is he going to push me off the cliff.

Is he seriously going to kill me?

"Are you going to push me off the cliff?" I hesitantly asked.

In response he laughed, a lot.

"You are so stupid" he said in between his laughs.

I agree with him.

I was confused.

Then he put a hand on my back and told me to come with him.

His hand sent sparks to my body.

When I reached the cliff, my eyes widen.

It was such a beautiful view, city lights can be seen from here. I can see whole city from here. And it's sunset time, which makes it look so mesmerizing. Why didn't I know such a place like it.

Because you are an unobserver.

"Because no one knows about this place" he answered my unasked question.

"I usually come here when I get frustrated and have a lots of stress on me I come here. I come here to make my mind free. I feel peace and happiness here" he said looking at me with softness in his eyes.

"Why are you telling me all this? I don't want to be rude but why did you bring me here?" I asked as I can't keep my mouth shut.

"I also don't know, just want you to be here with me" he smiled.

I also smiled in reply. His smile was contagious.

His face was looking even more beautiful in the dim lights. He slide an arm around my waist and pulls me closer.

He came closer and stared at me for sometime like I was the most beautiful thing in the world. He kissed my cheeks, first left then right, lastly forehead.

I close my eyes because of the unknown peace I'm getting in his arms.

Then he hold my hand and pull it toward his mouth and kissed the back of my palm.

My cheeks were surely red by now. I don't know what I'm feeling but I dont want this feeling to stop.

Suddenly I felt something cold on my finger. I instantly opened my eyes and saw a beautifully craved diamond ring on my finger.

He kissed on the ring.

Then smiled at me.

"This is my grandma's ring, she told me to put this ring on the right girl, the one whom I want to cherish and love my whole life and I don't think anyone else eould be more deserving than you " he said smilingly.

My heart skipped a beat.

I was staring at him in pure shock.

But he ignored me and pulled me into a tight hug.

I don't know what happened but I hugged him back.

After few moments of hug he pulled himself back, he was looking at my lips then he started getting closer.

I closed my eyes on instant.

But,

Our moment got interrupted by the ringing of his phone.

Damn!

He abruptly pulled away and excused himself to receive the call.

What's just happened?

He was about to kiss me.

And you were also about to kiss him.

I blushed hard.

After few minutes he came back and awkwardly said "Um, Scar... I have to go home. An urgent work came up. Sorry, but we have to go now" he said while scratching the back of his neck.

He's looking cute doing that.

I nodded as no words came from my mouth.

We reached his car got seated and drove towards my home.

The whole ride was silent. When we reached my home, he kissed my cheek and said goodbye to me and he soon drove off.

I entered my home and walked towards my room and changed into sleep-wear and lied down on my bed.

How will sleep come to me today?

Is Mr. Rude seriously Mr. Rude?

Another chapter completed...

Hope you guys like it..

Thanks for reading..

Do vote and comment...

Love y'all

28/03/2018

Chapter 15

E ros's attire above

Eros's POV

Last night was amazing as Scarlett finally agreed to marry me.

She didn't agreed, you made her agree.

Whatever. At the end she's marrying me.

I'm happy that I went to her home and met her.

My happy moment was interrupted by a phone call and the person was none other than by best friend, Nick Wilson.

I was ingnoring him since two days but now I think I have to attend this call.

"Hello" Nick said.

"Hey" I said.

"Where the heck were you and why are you not answering my calls? I'm such an ass that I'm wasting my precious time by calling you and you who choose to ignore all my calls, bloody hell" he hissed. And I kept my phone a little bit away from my ears otherwise he'll surely make me deaf.

"I was indulged in something" I replied.

"Wow man, what a reply. Seriously? That's what you only got? I know you are a bloody ceo but you should also know that I'm your only friend but no, you ignored me, you ignored your only best friend. What have I done to have a friend like you?" he spoke.

"Stop with your drama Nick. Now tell me what do you want?" I huffed.

"Drama? Really? You think all this is drama? You hurt me. You just punctured my poor heart. My best friend just hurt my feelings" he cried.

I groaned.

"Stop being a cry baby and tell me what do you want?" I questioned.

"Can't a best friend ask about his best friend? You are so mean. So how are you?" He asked.

"I'm fine" I replied.

"So? what's going on in your life?" He asked.

"Nothing much" I replied.

He sighed.

"You stupid arrogant rude man. How could you? Don't you have a heart and here I was thinking that I'm important to you but no, you proved me wrong. Oh Lord, I don't wanna live anymore in this world where my only best friend don't share things with me" he fake cried.

"What the hell happened to you?" I asked.

"You are getting married and you didn't even tell me, bro, I'm your best friend or was, I don't know. Still, you didn't tell me anything about you getting married. When we're you going to inform me? When you have became a father or a grandfather? Oh my lovely lord, take me away from him" he dramatically said.

I sighed.

"Who told you? Is that my mom?"

"It's not important, you didn't informed me. Leave it, and tell me who is the unlucky girl, who said yes to marry you? When is your engagment party man? Is your only best friend invited or not?" He questioned.

"She's a beautiful but crazy girl. Her name is Scarlett Miller. You'll soon meet her and I'm sure you'll also like her and the engagement ceremony is day after tomorrow and I know even if I don't invite you, you'll still come to the party. So you're with due respect are invited " I smiled.

"Yeah you are right, perks of a best friend. Wait a minute, how can you even think of not inviting me?" he huffed.

He's such a baby sometimes.

"Now stop your drama and be there on time, if you want to meet her and attend my engagement" I said.

"Okie dokie, by the way I want to meet the unlucky girl, who agreed to marry such a jerk like you" he teased.

I was about to reply but he hung my call. I'll deal with him later.

After few minutes my office room door flung open and my mom came with her toothy grin.

"Oh honey. I love you so much. I'm glad you find Scarlett perfect match for you and I know she also can't resist your charms.." my mom said smilingly.

Oh really? As much as I know she surely didn't fell for your charms.

"Why are you here mom? If you wanted something you should have told me. I would have given you a visit" I asked warily.

"Oh dear. I'm not that old and don't compare me with the oldies. I'm not became a grandmother yet " she laughed.

Grandmother?

"I came here to you give you your grandma's ring. Do you remember? This our family's heirloom and I want you to give it to Scarlett" she said giving me a box of ring.

When I opened it, a beautiful ring was there. I have seen it before but every time I see it I remember my grandma.

"Give this ring to the one whom you heart wants, whom you want to be your, whom you want to cherish and love your whole life"My grandma's words.I smiled at the memories.

"Okay mom I'll give it to her soon and mom I have told Scarlett that you'll go with them tomorrow for wedding shopping and did you tell Anna about the engagement and the wedding?" I asked.

Anna is my little sister who is studying right now in abroad and would be back soon.

"Yes dear I called her yesterday and told her about all the details. She was so excited for the wedding and to meet Scarlett and I'll surely go to Maril house tomorrow" she smiled.

"I think I should leave now, love you dear" she kissed my forehead and left.

I sighed.

When should I give this ring to her?

Why not today?

You're right today is perfect and I can meet her. I grinned.

Lover boy.

Let's get Scarlett's number first.

I called Maril, Scarlett's mom and asked Scarlett's number and her whereabouts.

She told me that she was in a cafe with her friends. She gavve me the address to the cafe.

I left my office telling Maya to postpone all the meetings and drove towards the cafe.

When I reached there I called her phone number but she didn't pick up.

After few attemps of calling she received the call but she didn't recognise me.

After telling her who I am, I literally forced her to come out. When she came out I was nit able to avert my gaze from her. She was looking so beautiful and hot in her attire. Every colour suits her.

After shamelessly checking her out I kissed her cheek and inhaled her sweet scent.

I opened the door for her and I too got seated and drove towards the place where I spend my most of the time alone.

But on the way I cane to know that she cant keep her mouth shut for a while. She likes to talk a lot. But I dont mind shutting her mouth. But when I told her or more like gave hint to her that how eoyld I shut her uo she kept her mouth shut for the rest of the drive.

When we reached our destination I heloed her to exit the car.

But when she saw the cliff I took her to, she asked me if I'm going to push her off.

I can't help but to laugh at her wired imagination.

She's so naive. How can even she think that?

"You are so stupid" I said in between my laugh.

After I controlled myself.

I put my hand on her back and told her to come with me.

When we reached the cliff her eyes widens.

It was indeed a beautiful view, city lights can be ed confusingly.

I seriously don't know why did I bring her here not even my family or friends but I want to show this place to her.

I told her about the place that no one knows about this place except me. And that I want her to see this place.

She was looking like an angel in dim lights. I slide an arm around her waist and pulled her closer.

I came close to her and kissed her cheeks, first left then right lastly her forehead.

Then I hold her hand and and kissed the back of her palm.

Her face was scarlet red by now. She looked even more beautiful while blushing.

Then I took out the ring from my pocket and slid it onto her finger.

Her eyes flew open in shock. She was looking at the ring.

I kissed the ring on her finger and smiled at her.

"This is my grandma's ring, she told me to put this ring on the right girl, the one whom I want to cherish and love my whole life and I don't think anyone else eould be more deserving than you" I said smilingly.

She was shocked by my sudden confession.

But I ignored her shocked state and pulled her into a tight hug.

And surprisingly she hugged me back.

Aww.. such a cute moment. She looks beautiful but only when she's calm.

After the hug, when I pulled back I was staring at her lips, not sure that I should kiss her kissable lips or not. I took the chance and moved forward. She immediately closed her eyes.

I was so close to her. So vlose to kiss her lips when my phone started ringing. I cursed under my breath and excused myself to answer the call.

The call was from Mr. Jenkins and he want the copy of file which was at my home. because of which I have to go home.

Damn! I was about to kiss her.

What is happening to me? Why can't I control myself around her? Something's wrong with me.

She was standing there blushing red.

I walked back to her and awkwardly told her that I have some urgent work and we have to head home now while scratching the back of my neck.

She nodded.

We reached my car got seated and drove towards her home.

The whole ride was silent, when we reached her home, I kissed her cheek and said goodbye to her and soon drove off.

After giving Mr. Jenkins the file I called it a night and went to my bedroom.

All night I was thinking about the kiss which never happened.

What will it be like to have her lips on mine?

Soon I'll know,

With that I slipped into dreams of Scarlett.

Another chapter completed...

Hope you guys like it..

Thank you all for reading...

Do vote and comment...

Love y'all

29/03/2018

Chapter 16

Nick's pic above

What do you think about it?

Do tell me

Scarlett's POV

As Eros said, the very next day his mom came and we went to buy the dress for engagement and other functions. We roamed around different stores.

We were totally exhausted when we came back home.

But her mother was a nice lady, not like Mr. Rude.

Still you like him.

No, I don't.

Keep on lying.

Today is my engagement ceremony and I'm getting ready for the function and my best friend Sonya was the one who is helping me to get ready.

I was wearing a red gown, with a slit which reaches my mid thigh. It was so beautiful. My makeup was minimal and she straightened my hairs and not to forget, heels.. my true love. I was wearing black heels. But no one can see them because my gown was so long.

Still I'm wearing it because I know about my heels that I'm wearing them.

You are totally obsessed with the heels, one day you're going to strain your neck with clumsy self.

I'm not that clumsy.

Yeah! And who is that girl who keeps on bumping people?

Okay, I got your point.

When I finally got ready, I glanced at the mirror. A gasp left my lips. I can't even recognize myself, I was looking different, like totally different. Never thought I can also look so glamorous.

All thanks to Sonya.

And me.

What did you do?

I stayed silent.

Right, thanks.

You owe me for that.

I rolled my eyes.

Soon my mom entered my room and her mouth broke into an ear to ear smile.

"Honey, you look exquisite. Red color suits you a lot" she said by kissing my forehead.

"Hey, I'm also here. What about me? Don't I look good" Sonya asked.

Sonya was wearing a light pink dress with her back open in a V cut. She looks beautiful and sexy as always with white heels.

"Yeah you also look very beautiful but not more than my daughter" my mom teased.

Sonya put an hand on heart showing that she was hurt and dramatically wiped her fake tears.

Drama queen.

I chuckled at both of them.

"Now let's get leaving, otherwise we'll be late and where is Richard?" My mom asked.

"Mom he'll be meeting us directly at the party" I said.

My mom nodded.

Then we all exited our house and got seated into the car and drove towards the location where my engagement party is held.

When we reached our destination I looked around sitting inside the car. The place was beautiful, lights were glowing everywhere, small lights were lit on the sides of road. It was totally a mesmerizing scene.

Wow, I didn't think that your engagement would be this good. Forget that, I don't even think that you'll get engaged one day. I thought you're going to die single.

Shut up.

Everyone exited the car except me as I was told that Eros and I have to enter together.

Romantic.

Yeah, yeah, why not? If you have to wait and can't even get out when you know that there is delicious, mouth watering food is getting eaten up by those hungry people, then only you can understand my feelings.

Poor you.

I was waiting in the car waiting for Eros to come when the car door opened. When I looked at the person, Eros. I look at him in an aww, he gawked at me for few seconds without blinking and was watching me like a hawk.

Guess someone got busy in checking you out.

Then he cleared his throat.

"Hello baby" he smiled.

He gave me his hand which I gladly accepted.

As I excited the car, Eros slide his hand around my waist and pulled me forward to kiss my cheek.

I turned red at his gesture,

When I turned my gaze towards him then only I noticed how handsomely sexy he was looking.

He was looking devilishly handsome in his black tux which was perfectly fitted to him and he was wearing a matching red bow tie to match my dress. He looked totally breathtakingly hot.

Oh my, he looks so dashing. How did you get so lucky?

When I came back to my senses after ogling him for don't know how much time, then only I noticed that he was checking me out and was looking at me, more like staring.

"You're looking totally ravishing tonight" he said with a wink.

I blushed,

"You also don't look bad yourself" I said.

A smile crept on his face.

Aww, this smile, the most beautiful thing. It should be banned, otherwise, I don't know how many people will die.

True.

When I looked forward dozens of cameramen were there to click our photos. Side effects of getting married to a CEO.

There were so many people shouting and clicking pictures of us, I got nervous and my body stiffens. Eros felt my discomfort, he hold my waist squeezing it a little like telling me everything's gonna be okay,

He helped me to tackle them all and we soon entered the hall like a perfect lovey-dovey couple.

Seriously he's your knight in the shining tux.

The hall was grand and beautifully decorated, lights were lit everywhere. It looks perfect, there were more than hundreds of people. The hall was fully packed.

Did everyone in this country got invited?

I took a deep breath and showed my best smile while entering and moved forward towards the crowd.

Don't smile to much people will think that you are oppressed by an evil power.

Shut Up!

"Attention everybody, the beautiful bride and handsome groom has arrived, give them a big round of applause, look how appealing they look hand in hand" someone announced.

Yeah, we are the star of the night.

And everyone turned their faces towards us and a chorus of claps and shouts started.

We both looked at each other and then faced towards the crowd and smiled.

Soon our family members joined us and started introducing to the guests.

There were so many guests that I got confused between their faces and their names, I am feeling like some kind of exam is taking place.

And you are surely failing it.

"So you are the one" an unknown voice said from behind me. When I turned around he was already looking me from up to down like approving of something. He was wearing a blue tux, his hair were light brown and his eyes were a very beautiful shade of Grayish blue, all over he looked cute.

Isn't he hot?

Yeah, but not more than Eros.

Seriously? Now you're comparing others with him.

"Huh?" I asked not knowing what he was saying.

"You are that girl whom my idiot of a friend trapped her in his charms? " he murmured to himself while grazing his chin,

"Sorry?" I asked.

"How can he be that lucky? You can do much more better than him, then why him. It's not that good looking guys are dead, then why he?" he asked to me now in more audible voice.

"Oh shut up"someone said from behind.

When I turned around Eros was coming towards our way.

Did he said shut up to you?

"Don't you dare say anything rubbish to my fiance otherwise I'll punch your not so good looking face" Eros said to the unknown guy.

"Okay, anything rubbish" he said with a shrug.

I laughed at his response. Eros rolled his eyes, the guy smiled at me and did a manly hug with Eros.

"How can you be so stupid?" Eros asked the guy.

"I don't know. That's my talent bro that not everybody have and I know you are jealous of me. It's not like the first time that I'm meeting my haters" the guy shrugged.

"So Scarlett? Why did you said yes to marry this idiot? Why not someone more intelligent than him or polite, he's so rude and mean" the guy said the last part whispering.

"Don't tell me you also fell for his charms and good looks?" he said shockingly.

I chuckled at his words, he sounds funny. How is he related to Eros?

"No. I didn't fell for his charms-" I said but got cut off by Eros

"She fell on her butts" he said teasingly.

Both of them laughed at this.

I groaned and narrowed my eyes at Eros. He shrugged.

Well technically, its the truth.

I know.

"On a serious note, why this idiot why not anyone with blue eyes and brown hair? Who must be near you or may be in front of you" he said.

I laughed. And shook my head.

"That's enough Nick" Eros huffed.

What's with him?

The cute guy laughed.

"Sorry I forgot to introduce myself, I'm Nick Wilson. This idiot's best friend. I have heard a lot about you Scarlett but the words don't do justice on you" Nick said by kissing the back of my palm.

I blushed.

"I bet he didn't tell you anything about me" Nick asked.

I shook my head telling him no he didn't.

"Ah, what can I say he's so possessive over me. He don't want people to know about me. They might steal me" he dramatically said with a wink at me.

I chuckled.

Eros's arm came around my waist and he pulled me towards him.

"No, I'm not possessive over you" Eros stated.

"What can I say? Priority changes" Nick said teasingly looking at Eros's arm.

I blushed.

"Scarlett I must say he got really lucky to have you, you'd be perfect for him. And please tell him to respect me because I'm his only friend. More like only one who can bear him" Nick grinned.

I laughed at this.

"Thank you Nick and I'll try to tell him about your importance" I smiled.

Suddenly someone called me.

When I turned towards the source of voice my best friends were calling for me.

I smiled back and walked towards them and hugged them both and introduced them to both Eros and Nick.

Eros excused himself and went away. Nick was such a nice guy, not anything like Mr. Rude. How can they be best friends?

When I looked around, I found Eros was talking to a very beautiful girl, with brown hair and hazel eyes. She was so beautiful. She was wearing a light purple evening gown in which she looks stunning. I was not able to avert my eyes from both of them.

Eros and I made an eye contact but soon he broke it and started talking to the girl like I don't even exist.

I huffed in annoyance.

I'm his fiance and he's ignoring me. Why the hell it is affecting me? He can talk to who so ever he want but why this unknown feeling? Something must be wrong with me.

I groaned.

Honey this unknown feeling is jealously.

No, it can't be. For jealousy I have to like him first which I don't think ever's gonna happen.

Liar. You obviously like him.

I don't think so.

I ignored my inner voices and Eros both and walked away from there to Richie.

"Who is that girl with Eros? Don't you think she's beautiful? " Richie asked eyeing the girl.

"I don't know, but don't you think Eros is very much engrossed and enjoying talking to her? Who the hell is she for whom he ignored me?" I huffed.

Why sudden anger, huh?

"Babe, don't take your anger on me. I know you're jealous but leave us " he said.

"Who told you I'm jealous because I'm not" I hissed.

"Yes you are. Even an blind can tell that you are so jealous of that girl" I groaned.

"I'm not and why would I be? Now excuse me" I grimly smiledand walked away.

When I was walking I bumped into a wall, a wall in the middle? Shit...shitty shit, tons of shit.

Don't you think it would be so much of shit? It's not a good thing to collect.

Keep quiet.

"Do you love to bump into me every time we're together?" He chuckled.

Why always he? Can't I bump into a real wall? It would be so much better.

Nope, poor wall will break.

"Er.. no, why would I? Actually I was in deep thoughts that's why I didn't see you" I replied.

"What were you thinking so deeply?" he questioned raising his eyebrow.

"None of your business" I snapped.

He sighed.

"Come I want you to meet someone very close to me" he said.

He must be taking you to that girl so he's so close to her.

"Um.. no I have to do something" I hurriedly walked out from there without even glancing back. I can hear him calling me.

I took a flute of champagne and gulped it down due to nervousness.

"Well hello there shortcake" Nick came in front of me.

I smiled and kept on walking.

"What happened? Why are you ignoring me? Did something happened to you? Everything's alright?" He asked.

"Uh... nothing, everything's fine" I said.

"Did Eros do anything?" He asked.

I kept quiet, he must have understood something that's why he suggested me this idea,

"Do you want to take a revenge on Eros?" He asked.

"Huh?" I confusingly asked.

"Yes or no?" He questioned.

This is the chance, accept his offer. He'll help you.

"I'm not sure, um... okay, but what are you going to do?" I hesitantly asked.

"Just wait and watch shortcake, we're going to have fun" he said with a wink.

He get a hold of my hand and walked in the middle of the hall.

"Let's make him jealous" he stated.

"What are you going to do? It will not harm him? It's for fun, right?" I questioned.

"Yes shortcake. Why would I hurt him? He's my best friend but we should give him some dose." he stated.

"What?"

This time he ignored me.

What is he trying to do?

How will Eros be jealous for me.

Oh god.

Did I do the right thing to accept Nick's proposal?

Another chapter completed...

Thank you all for reading..

Hope you guys like it..

Do vote and comment...

Love y'all

30/03/2018

Chapter 17

Anna's pic above..

What do you think?

Do tell

Scarlett's POV

The music started playing.

"Would you give me the pleasure of dancing with such a beautiful lady tonight?" Nick asked.

"Umm..." I started but he cut me off.

"Please, only this one. I insist" he said by fluttering his eyes.

I chuckled. How can anyone say no to him?

"Sure" I smiled.

He put his one hand on my waist and used another to hold my hand. I put my one hand on his shoulder and one in his hand.

Then we started moving ourselves according the music.

"You know? Eros is shooting daggers at me. He must be planning of killing me. If I die please tell the cruel world I'm the best friend anyone can in this world" he stated.

I raised my eyebrow.

"And why would he do that?" I asked.

"Why don't you see by your own?" He smiled.

When I looked behind Eros was seriously shooting daggers at Nick. He was getting annoyed.

He looks mad.

"Yes. You're right, but why?" I asked.

"You are so naive shortcake. He likes you a lot and he won't tell you but I can surely tell you that and till now he must be fuming in anger. We just have to wait for the smoke coming out from his ears" he chuckled.

I laughed.

"He don't like me and he's doing this marriage thing because of his ego and his mom's pressure nothing else " I stated.

"To tell you the truth and to open your eyes, I'm putting my life in danger. You'll be thankful to me in future for what I did" he said.

"Now he'll soon come here and will take you away from me or more like snatch you away" he said.

"I appreciate your effort but I don't think he is gonna do that" I said.

"Just wait and watch, shortcake" he said.

In not more than a minute, we were interrupted by none other than Mr. Rude himself.

Wow! Nick's right, he did came.

"Have you both done your dancing and talking? Can I take my fiance back if you don't mind? " he grimly smiled.

"Of course, she's all yours. I was just being a gentleman " Nick said shrugging innocently.

"Shortcake don't feel bad for the interruption by this fiance of yours, I'll soon come and get you" he teased.

"Nick " Eros growled.

I chuckled.

"Dude, I was just kidding. She's yours" he said and left with a wink.

He was right. He did came and interrupted our dancing.

This means he likes you?

May be.

Eros hold my waist with his both hands and pulled me closer towards him. I gasped at the sudden pull but I put both my hands on his shoulders to make some distance between us. My heartbeats increase at our closeness.

Again this stupid feelings, why does it all come when he's around me?

You know, it can be acidity.

Shut up!

"You know, you should dance with me first as I'm your fiance" he said, interrupting my argument with my inner voice.

I rolled my eyes, as if he was waiting for me to dance with him first,

"Yeah, I would have liked to dance with you but you are busy with your very VIP guests " I said with the most fake smile I can gather.

"And who would that be?" He asked.

I narrowed my eyes at him.

Is he going to act innocent now?

"Don't act innocent, you know very well whom I was talking about. You were busy in talking to a girl, like only she matters to you " I said but the last line came without my consent.

Please now go and bump into a real wall this time,

He smirked.

"So my dear fiance is jealous huh?"he said by dipping his face in the crook of my neck,

I shuddered because of his breath fanning across my neck, so I pushed him and walked away from him.

Why would I be jealous?

Why is everyone saying that?

I don't care about him.

He can talk to whosoever he wants to talk.

I walked away. I don't want to listen stupid things that I'm jealous etc etc.

I busied myself in attending the guests when from no where Sonya came.

"Scar, I've been looking for you like hell, where were you?" She asked.

"I was here only, what happened to you? And why are you searching for me?" I questioned.

"Forget that. Your mom has been asking for you from everyone"she said.

"Mom? What? Why? What happened?" I asked.

"Uh.. I don't know but you should go to her as soon as possible, she's getting impatient" she said.

"Where is she?" I asked.

"Uhh, come with me" she said and guided me to where my mom is. I excused myself from the guests and followed Sonya. We reached a corridor which have a few rooms. She took me to one room and told me that my mom will be in this room.

Why would your mom be in this room?

How do I know? Let's meet her then only we can find whats wrong.

Sonya left after telling me.

I entered the room and the room was dark.

"Mom?" I asked in the dark. I walked further into the room but no response came, so I decided to go back to the hall.

As I was about to go,

From nowhere a hand crept on my waist.

I blanched, my eyes opens like saucers I started screaming like a maniac. But one hand came to my mouth shutting me up.

Oh my God, I'm dying and my death will occur due to a ghost.

Suddenly the hand pulled me and pushed my back towards the door.

Then the lights lit up,

And a pair of green eyes came into my view.

Huh? The ghost also have green eyes? Why do all green eyed people comes to you?

But why does this ghost seems similar like Eros?

Because he is Eros.

Oh!

Why is he here.? Where's mom? Sonya said mo- Uhh! Sonya, I'm going to kill you for this, you'll be dead.

"Wha d el wr uu thikin" I tried to talk but his hand was covering my mouth.

"What?" He confusingly asked.

I rolled my eyes.

I pointed my finger towards my mouth where he had put his hand and forgot to remove it.

"Oh! Now tell what were you saying?" He said after removing his hand.

"What the hell were you doing here? I was scared like hell. I thought I'll die on my engagement day, God! What were you even thinking of doing this stupid act? I know you're stupid but I don't imagined that you'll be this.." I was cut of by his finger on my lips.

"Oh God! Why do you speak so much? Can't you just keep your mouth shut for a while? I shouldn't have removed my hand from your mouth" He muttered annoyingly.

He then sighed and took a deep breath like he's calming himself.

"Now tell me, why did you ran away? When you were dancing with me?" He asked by tightening his grip on my waist.

"What?" I asked trying to be innocent.

He started sliding his fingertips on my arm, an unknown feeling ran through me. A different sensation in the pit of my stomach. What is he doing to me?

I cleared my throat.

"I-I didn't ran away, uh.. mm... I have to do something that's why, yeah... that's why I left" I said by a nod with head.

"Oh! Is that so? I thought you felt uncomfortable or more like jealous because I was talking to someone else which you didn't like or so?" he said huskily,

And how dare he? How dare he put that topic up? I don't wanna talk on that topic but no, uhh.

He was now touching my cheeks with his hands, uhh, I was melting in his touch but, I have to control.

"No, n-not at all, why would I feel jealous, whether you talk to any woman or man? Why would I care? No, I don't care if you are talking to a very beautiful girl, who looks stunning and you kept on talking to her like there's no tomorrow, even if you ignore me while talking to someone else. I don't feel anything for you, you keep on dreami..." I was cut off by his lips on mine.

Oh my gooooooooooddddddddd!!!

My eyes widen.

A spark ran through my body.

HE IS KISSING ME!!

He started moving his lips against mine passionately. I closed my eyes on instant, he nibbled on my lower lip and asked for entrance. I was melting under his touch but didn't opened my mouth.

He lowered his hand and grabbed my butt, which caused me to yelp and with which he took the opportunity and shoved his tongue in my mouth. He touched every inch of my mouth with his tongue.

I don't know what came into me. I moved my hands and put them in his soft and silky hairs.

I moaned in his mouth.

I'm loving this feeling.

Due to lack of oxygen he moved his lips from mine and moved downwards towards my neck, he showered kisses onto my neck which caused me to moan. After assaulting my neck for sometime, he again put his lips on mine.

Our sweet moment was interrupted by a knock.

We instantly pulled away, we both were out of breath.

He looked at me, I blushed. My cheeks turned red.

Someone again knocked on the door.

Eros clearer his throat before answering, "Yes?" He asked.

"Bro? Are you in? Everyone's looking for you, come downstairs" Nick's voice came from other side.

Eros replied to him still looking at me and I turned my gaze down the floor. Isn't the carpet nice?

Yeah sure.

"Okay. I'm coming" Eros said.

With that Nick walked away as I heard his footsteps.

"Let's go downstairs, otherwise our mom will send a searching team to find us " he said.

I nodded and started walking towards the door.

He put his hand on my back as we exited the room.

When we reached downstairs Sonya was looking at our side, smirking.

Traitor,

I narrowed my eyes at her showing you-will-be-dead look.

She just shrugged.

Eros took me towards a group of people.

We walked there and the same purple dressed girl came face to face with me,

What is she doing here?

She hurriedly came to me and engulfed me in a tight hug.

Don't tell me she's also a bone crusher.

"You are more beautiful in personal. Oh god! I'm so happy, I can't believe my rude brother is going to marry someone. I thought no one's going to marry him. Finally I'll also have a sister, who's so beautiful. Eros's so lucky." she said while jumping and squealing.

Sister?

"Meet my little sister Anna" he said with a smirk.

I froze on my spot.

What the shitter's shit!

She's his sister.

And you even told him that you were jealous.

Oh my god!!

Why this always happens to me?

I want to hide in my bed under my minions duvet and I promise I won't peek, but please someone hide me.

Now I can notice the similarities both have, why am I so stupid? Why did I said everything to Eros.

Eros was chuckling at my situation.

I really want to cry.

I took a deep breath and replied Anna,

"Nice to meet you too Anna. I'm also happy that I'll also have a cute sister like you. Now we'll both have our girly time" I smilingly said.

"Aww, you are too damn good for him" she said.

I blushed.

Suddenly very nice track started playing.

"Would you like to have a dance with me, Miss Miller who is soon to be Mrs. Jordan?" Eros asked.

I smiled as everyone's around. I can't even say no in front of everyone.

"I'd love to, Mr. Jordan" I replied.

He took me to the dance floor.

And we started dancing with the beats of the music.

This time we both were too close to each other, out chests were touching,

"Why didn't you tell me that she's your sister?" I annoyingly asked.

"You didn't gave me a chance to tell the you about her, like I have told you jump on conclusions without even listening to other's views" he said.

He twirled me around.

"You should have told me, somehow" I said.

"No, if I would have told you, then, I won't get a chance to kiss your delicious lips " he teased.

I blushed red.

I lowered my gaze.

He chuckled and tightened his grip on my waist.

"You look so cute when you blush, soon to be Mrs. Jordan " he said with a kiss on my cheek.

"Awwww, look at them, they look so cute together" Sonya commented.

"Thank you so much Sonya. I owe you" Eros said.

I narrowed my eyes at Sonya.

"Surely and babe don't get angry sometimes someone have to play the cupid's role" she said with a wink at me.

I rolled my eyes.

After a few minutes of dancing, me and mom left for our home.

Today's flashback came into my mind when I lied down on my bed.

The kiss.

I can still feel the touch of his lips on mine. He's such a good kisser.

I touched my lips with my fingers.

Why did I like it so much?

What's happening to me?

What are you doing to me Mr Rude?

Another chapter completed.

I hope you all like it.

Thanks for your love and support.

Keep voting and commenting.

I love you all

01/04/2018

Chapter 18

Thank you everyone for your love and support.

Your support inspires me to write more.

Keep reading and don't forget to tell me about the chapter.

Enjoy

Scarlett's POV

My wedding shopping was going on a great rush.

I have to go to the designer and give my measurements and to buy various dresses for the wedding functions almost daily.

As the days are passing I'm getting nervous about what will happen at the wedding?

You'll get married to Eros. Duh. What are you thinking what'll happen?

I rolled my eyes.

I know that I'm going to marry Eros.

And the most amazing thing is that my wedding is day after tomorrow so that I'll have full day for myself to rest.

Today we all have planned to celebrate my last days as a bachelorette, so Sonya and Richie planned a party at a club. I am not at all interested in celebrating but what can I do.

Yeah, you are a bore type. Who can sleep the whole day on her last days as a bachelorett.

Shut up. That's the best thing anyone can do.

I have to agree as both my friends were showing their puppy faces. How could I have said no to them?

So today I chose to wear a black strapless dress, whose upper portion is filled with sequins.With my favourite red heels. smokey black eyes and redlipstick.

I was admiring myself in the mirror as I did all the make up by myself.

Damn! I look sexy, I totally did a great job. I didn't know I was gifted.

Unexpected from you but I think God is with you that's why you didn't turn yourself into a clown.

Sonya came into my room or more like barged in.

"Wow, you look hot in that black dress, He won't able stop himself" she complimented.

Who's he?

"He?" I questioned.

"Uh nothing. I'm saying that everyone in the club will have their eyes on you, I'm so excited" she said.

"Oh, I don't look that nice"I blushed.

"You too look stunning, even more than me" I replied.

"Thanks babe. But it's your day today. Now let's leave, Richie is waiting for us in the car, if we don't reach on time he'll surely get mad and mad Richie is not a good Richie" she said.

Why am I feeling that your friend has planned something?

No, you're exaggerating.

I still asked her.

"Sonya? Eros is not coming there, right?" I questioned by narrowing my eyes at her.

"Noo, pfft..not at all, what would he be doing there? He have his own party to attend. I don't think he's coming. Now hurry up, we're getting late" she said.

I hope everything wents well.

With a last glance at mirror we exited my room.

"You are looking so hot. I should have tried on you, your bad"Richie said with a whistle.

I punched his shoulder.

"Oww, you punch like a man" he cried. I once again puched him.

He rubbed his shoulder where I hit him.

I chuckled.

We got seated in the car and drove towards the club.

The club was fully packed with people, loud music was playing, neon lights were making my vision go blind. But still it was fun to be in such an atmosphere.

We entered and reached towards our booth. Where we all got seated and ordered our drinks.

Sonya excused herself from us and left for her touch ups.

"I can't believe you are getting married, our stupid little Scarlett is going to become a wife. Someone selected our stupid friend to get married, God save his poor soul from you" Richie fake cried.

I rolled my eyes.

Such great friends I have.

"Oh shut up" I rolled my eyes.

Soon our drinks arrived so as Sonya, I took a sip of my drink.

"Wow, this drink tastes nice, what is it?" I took another sip.

"Just enjoy the drink babe, don't ask just drink. After all it's your bache-lorett party" she winked.

"Hello everyone" a voice came from behind. When I looked there, Anna was standing their grinning.

Sonya waved back and told her to come our way.

I didn't know she was coming? But I didn't invited her so who?

"Me" Sonya said.

Did I said that loud?

"Yup" Sonya said.

Okay.

I got up and hugged Anna.

"Thanks for coming, it meant a lot to me" I smiled at her.

"No problem, I wanted to be here. I was getting bored sitting at home doing nothing" she smiled back.

Look she also gets bored sitting at home.

Everyone is different.

You're not different. You're one of a kind.

Is that a compliment?

Well it's not but you can take it in whatever way you want.

Get lost.

Anna got seated and ordered her drink.

After talking for sometime with Anna, I found she's a very sweet and polite girl, totally opposite of her brother, Eros.

How can anyone be jealous of her?

I know. I'm stupid.

Suddenly my vision started to blurr, what is happening to me, is it the drink? No, Sonya knows I don't drink because I do stupid things after that.

I shaked my head to clear my view.

"Babe, let's go to dance floor and let's have fun, after all it's my bff's bachelorette party" Sonya winked and dragged me to the dance floor.

Richie and Anna didn't came, they wanted to have a few more drinks before joining us for dancing.

Love is in the air.

I started swaying my hips according to the music and started dancing on the beat as soon as I reached the dance floor.

After a few minutes of dancing I found similar green looking at me in admiration.

Doesn't he looks like Eros?And look Nick is also with him.

But why would they be here? Sonya told us that they won't be coming. I'm totally hallucinating.

They are not them. My mind is playing games with me. And my inner voice is helping my mind in fooling me.

The duplicate Eros came towards me and hugged me.

Why is he hugging you?

"Woah man stay away, don't touch me. I'm engaged to someone. Can't you see the ring" I pushed him away and raised my hand to show my ring.

"Scar, are you alright?" he asked.

The duplicate even knows your name.

"Yes I'm fine, but keep distance from me " I grinned.

Why the hell you are grinning?

I don't know. I can't stop myself.

"If you don't mind can I dance with you and it'll be only dancing no touching, I promise" the guy said.

I don't think one dance with this hot guy would hurt.

"Okay, only dancing" I told him.

He nodded.

Soon we started dancing to the beat.

I can't help but think, isn't the guy looks just like Eros, too sexy, too hot, too charming, too Eros, I raised my hand and touched his cheek.

"You know you look exactly like my Mr. Rude, the one whom I'm getting married" I told him while dancing.

"Oh I see. Are you happy to marry Mr. Rude?" He asked.

"Don't know" I shrugged.

"Then why are you marrying me.. um..Mr. Rude" he questioned.

Suddenly I felt sad.

"I have to otherwise he'll break my mom's and her best friend's bond" I sadly replied..

"So you hate him?" He asked.

No, why would I hate him? Do I?

No babes, you like him.

A smile came on my face.

"No, I don't hate him, he's rude, arrogant, annoying, stubborn and insane but I like him. Don't know why but can't control myself from liking him. He's not that bad" I stated.

"Do you know him?" I asked.

He shaked his head in no.

"That's good. May be if you know him you'll also fall for his charms and let me tell you one thing mister I don't share" I told him by narrowing my eyes at him.

I can see the duplicate blushing. But why would he? I let it go.

"And why would I fall for him?" The duplicate asked.

I actioned him with my hands to come near.

I got closer to his ear and told him "You know he's very smart and sexy, sometimes I drool over him, but because of his arrogance and rudeness I named him Mr. Rude" I giggled.

"This name suits him a lot. I'm so good at giving names to people" I laughed and patted my back.

"Don't tell this to him otherwise he'll be on the seventh heaven, that I praised him" I told him with a giggle.

Why can't I stop giggling.

Because you are stupid.

I know I am.

I again giggled.

He smiled his toothy smile.

Wow he also have a beautiful smile.

Just like Eros.

"Lets get seated somewhere, I like talking to you, you're an interesting guy" I literally dragged him to the bar area and we got seated.

The duplicate was staring me constantly.

"One martini for me, do you want anything?" I asked the guy.

He shaked his head in no.

"Why did you agreed to get married to him?" Duplicate guy questioned.

"You know Mr. Rude forced me into this marriage. At first I didn't like it at all but now I'm looking forward to it. Every girl wants his hubby to be too damn sexy as him. I want to say no to him but.." I said.

A slow smile crept on his face.

I continued.

"Whenever I'm with him I'm always in a different trance and when he kissed me. Wow.. just wow, fireworks started in my body. Kissing him is an amazing feeling" I said by taking a sip of my drink.

"So you like his kisses?" He asked.

"Who would not like them? He's a pro. Totally awesome" I told him.

"I think he's a lucky guy to have you, you are so beautiful, young and cute" he smilingly said.

He's finding you cute. May be he's also drunk.

Shut up.

"Mr. Rude should be like you, you are so sweet. If I don't have to marry him I would have surely married you. Because you look just like Eros. My fiancé" I said by pulling his cheeks.

He smiled at me.

I suddenly started feeling dizzy. I gripped my seat tightly.

"Are you okay?" Duplicate asked.

"Yeah, just a bit dizzy." I replied holding my head.

"I think we should head home" he stated.

I nodded.

He paid the bill and held me by shoulders and walked with me to the exit.

He took me to his car and got seated. A very familiar fragrance came into my nostrils.

"You smell very nice. Just like Eros, are you Eros? But how can you be him? He must be enjoying his bachelor's party with some beautiful, hot and sexy girls "I murmered.

"Seriously you don't recognise me?" He muttered under his breath but I heard him.

He glanced at me then back on road.

Don't you have a feeling that he is Eros?

I also feel the same, if he's Eros why did I rambled everything to him?

Because You are stupid as I told you.

I think then it's better if I don't recognise him.

When we reached home I was very sleepy. I think I must have created a nice music by bumping my head against the car interiors.

"Are you able to walk?" He questioned.

I nodded. When I got up I stumbled and was about to fall but was grabbed by the guy.

He swiftly carried me in his arms and took me to my home.

I burried my face into his chest, umm..

"You really smell very nice. Can you suggest Mr. Rude the same cologne?" I deeply inhaled his scent.

"Sure" he replied.

He entered my room and placed me on my bed and got seated beside me.

"You look very cute when you are drunk "he said by touching his fingers along my body.

He came closer and was looking at me like he was remembering my facial features, he was so close to me. Ah! He's so handsome.

An unknown feel came into me and I wanted to be in his arms, wanted to touch him, feel him.

I put both my hands around his neck and asked "Can I kiss you?"

I can't control myself. I was in different frenzy, deep down I know he was none other than Eros I have a strong feeling about it.

He shocks for a second but soon obliged my request and put his lips on mine.

Sparks ran through my body in a lightening speed.

Goosebumps rose all over my body. I can't get enough of his kisses. He's totally a pro, my soon to be husband.

He deepens the kiss, his one hand was on my cheek and other was balancing him.

Soon he pulled away when we both ran out of oxygen. He stood up and was about to go.

Why is he going? I don't want him to go.

So I grabbed his hand.

"Eros? " I whispered.

He turned around and looked at me intently.

"Please stay" I requested.

He thought for a minute, then he nodded and sat beside me and kissed my forehead.

He helped me to lie down on my bed and covered me with my duvet.

"Good night Scarlett" he said.

He lied beside me and tightly hugged me and burried his face in my neck, he inhaled deeply and planted butterfly kisses.

"Can't wait to get married to you, only one day left" he said.

"Then you'll be mine"

Was the last words I heard.

I soon was in a deep oblivion.

Hello lovely readers..

Thank you all for reading

I hope you like the chapter

Keep on commenting and voting

Love you all

03/04/2018

Chapter 19

Scarlett's POV

I groaned and rubbed my eyes to remove the excess sleep from my eyes.

My head was throbbing in pain, like someone was hammering my head.

I had a stupid dream last night.

Where I told Eros to kiss me.

Why would I do that?

Pfftt.

I laughed at my stupid thoughts.

Why would I kiss him and will request him to stay?

I snorted.

I have to do something for this pain, ughh, its making me insane.

You already are.

Shut up.

I got up from my bed and took two aspirin and then went to bathroom and did my morning rituals.

When I came back to my room I see a note sitting on the side table.

What's that?

I picked it up and started reading it.

"Sorry for not staying with you as you requsted as I don't want to invade your privacy, but don't worry, I'll make sure that soon I'll be with you on OUR bed. Only one day left Scarlett.

P.S. you look cute when you are drunk and I'll not tell anything about Mr. Rude to him.

Love,Eros

Was he really here?

No someone came and put this letter for you so that you'll go running around in happiness that he came.

Oh shut up.

I started recalling yesterday's events.

I remember going to the club with both Sonya and Richie. Then Anna joined us. The drinks, then we danced a lot and then,

Similar pair of green eyes..

Bloody hell!!

Mr. Rude.

Means he was there?

Damn!

This means that kissing thing which I thought was a dream, was not actually a dream.

How can be so stupid?

Because you are.

Oh my pet's shit!!

Hey you don't have a pet.

Yeah, but my neighbour has.

Oh my neighbour's pet's shit!!

Omg! I really asked him to kiss me, and all the things that I rambled about Eros. I was actually saying all that to Eros.

How can I be so dumb? I should have known that he's the same Eros.

I facepalmed myself.

Seriously I didn't expected all that from you. I know you're stupid but that much stupid, never imagined. You proved me wrong.

You were also there, you could have told me, so you can't blame only me.

I'm your inner voice, you should not be so dependent on me.

Aargh!

My head is hurting like hell. I don't wanna wake up yet and face the world. I want to sleep.

Why did I agree to go to that damn club, I shouldn't have gone there.

Suddenly my room burst open and Sonya barged in.

"Hello soon to be Mrs. Jordan. How are you feeling. You know its already afternoon and you're still not up yet? You know you're getting married tomorrow. Wakey wakey" She shouted.

"Shut up Sonya, first this stupid beating of drums in my head and now you. Both of you can't stop yourselves. I feel like hell...please turn your voice down" I told her.

"I didn't think that drink will give you hungover, it was not that strong" she said while thinking.

"No, its not that drink, I drink more after that...wait, what? What do you mean by the drink will give me hangover? Sonya what did you do this time?" I asked by narrowing my eyes.

My Lord, she's the culprit of you headache, she should be punished by a cold bucket of water.

"Um.. that's was just to make you enjoy the party and come out from your World and have fun" she said.

"I was enjoying the party and you know that when I drink I do stupid things. Everytime I drink I make a fool out of myself. You should've known Sonya" I told her.

"I'm sorry I never knew this would happen, now forget it and tell me what happened after you left from there with Eros, tell me everything in detail" she excitedly asked.

"Do you anyhow know? Why did Eros came at the same club where we're already partying?" I questioned.

"No, no, I don't know, I didn't do anything. I didn't even tell Nick our location. I'm sure it's a coincidence" she closed her mouth with her hands..

I glared at her. I'm really gonna kill her.

"How could you Sonya? You're my best friend and now you're planning against me, you very well know I don't like him still you betrayed me, why?" I huffed and crossed my arms in front of my chest.

She is on your side or him? I doubt that.

"Babe, firstly you were looking damn hot that every guy was drooling over you and second Eros should know how hot and sexy you are. And how beautiful are you. I wanted to show him that he's lucky to have you not the other way around" she replied.

I sighed.

"Forget that, tell me the juicy details about yesterday" she again asked.

"Nothing much he left me in my room and then made me sleep and then he left" I told her.

Last night memories came into my mind which make my cheeks go red. That kiss..

"What are you not telling me? Wait, am I seeing right? You're blushing, oh my gosh! Tell me everything" she stated by narrowing her eyes.

I blushed hard.

Then I told her everything about yesterday night leaving the details where I asked him to kiss me.

We both spent our day together while finalizing everything for my wedding.

I'm going to marry Eros,

I hope everything goes well.

~~~~(The Wedding Day)~~~~
~~~~

Next day I woke up early as I have to get myself ready for my wedding.

H

urry up my soldier, your wedding is waiting ahead for you to attend.

All the stylists and the make up artists reached on time and started doing my make up.

I started feeling nervous. But Sonya supported me by boosting my confidence.

"Every thing will be fine and you are going to kick everyone's butt" she said with a squeeze on my shoulder.

I smiled at her.

After I don't know how many hours my make up and hair was done.

I wore my wedding dress, when I came out after wearing the dress, everyone was looking at me in with their mouth hung open.

"Honey, you look gorgeous. I wish your dad was also with us" my mom said first by kissing my forehead.

I can see her eyes watering.

I hugged her tightly and controlled the river flow through my eyes.

"Hey I also love to crush others in a hug, don't forget me. I'm also coming" Sonya said and came forward and embraced both mom and me.

She seriously crushed every single bone.

I finally took a glance at the mirror, OMG... I can't recognise myself. I was looking totally different in the white dress that I'm wearing.

You are actually looking beautiful. stylists did a nice job in renovating your face. I thought your face was unrepairable.

The upper portion of my dress was embedded with silver sparkly stones, my hair was done in a bun and some hair were left out of the bun, with smokey eyes, diamond earings which were totally matching my dress. I wore silver 5 inch heels which looks perfect..heels.

"Seriously Scar you look alluring. Eros will be fainting for sure and I'm gonna capture that moment " she teased.

Blush crept on my cheeks.

My look was finally completed with a long veil.

When I turned around I can see both mom's and Sonya's eyes watery.

I'm also gonna cry, do you have some tissues? Please don't tell anyone that I cried.

Why are YOU crying?

Because they all are crying.

"Hey don't start waterfall now. Otherwise I'll also start my tap, which will not stop soon and my make-up will get ruined" I warned them.

They chuckled.

Soon Richie entered in my room yelling.

"When is the bride going to be ready? I'm really getting hungry. When will I have the delicious food. I know whatever the bride will do she'll still look like a monkey, she.." he trailed off when he looked towards me.

He stared me from up to down.

"Wow!! You look beautiful. I-I know, you're not my Scar, where is she? She isn't this beautiful, she was like a monkey and she also punchs like a man"he teased.

I punched his shoulder.

"Oww! Okay, okay, don't need to be violent. I get it, you are our Scarlett, who punch like a man" he said rubbing his shoulder.

I rolled my eyes.

"Jokes apart, Scar you look damn stunning. Eros is a one lucky guy" he said with a kiss on my cheek.

I rubbed my cheek with an eww.

"Hey, girls die to get a kiss from me" he huffed.

"No, it's more like girls die after getting a kiss from you" I stuck my tongue out at him.

He chuckled and rolled his eyes.

"Time for crushing each other" Sonya said by grabbing us all in a tight hug.

Are your ribs okay?

We all laughed at Sonya's childishness.

She is totally a strong woman.

After our hugging ceremony we all left for the venue.

Richie would be walking with me down the aisle, as my father's no more so Richie insisted to walk with me. I literally crushed him in a hug when he said that, I'm glad to have a friend like him.

When we reached the venue my heart was beating like drums. Everyone could hear my drums.. I mean my heartbeats.

I was very nervous to go there, as it was my first time.

Seriously first time, are you going to marry like zillion times?

Hey I'm nervous.

Someone opened my car's door and I can see Richie's hand. I held his hand and exited the car,

Breathe in, breath out.

The music started playing and my heart was beating like it would come out of my body and will accuse me for giving him so much pressure.

I placed my arms in Richie's and started walking.

We slowly slowly walked towards the stage. I was walking carefully as I don't want everyone to laugh at my falling. Richie squeezed my hand in assurance.

I took a glance of the surroundings. I was mesmerized by the view, the place was looking so beautiful, everything was decorated in white colour, white flowers, white chairs, white flower petals were spread on my way, which was giving me a real princess like feel.

It felt like a dream, how can real world be so beautiful?

While glancing everywhere through the crowd, similar green orbs caught my gaze.

Eros.

He was looking so hot and dashing in his black tux, white shirt, he was staring at me with an intense gaze, which made my cheeks go red.

How can even a person look so damn perfect. he's like a greek god whom god sent just for you.

He smiled at me.

I lowered my gaze and kept on walking.

God help me to not to do anything stupid, let the wedding compelte in a normal way without my clumsiness.

I too wish the same.

Fingers crossed.

Hello lovelies..

Hope you are liking the chapter..

Do tell me about your views..

Soon Scarlett is going to be Mrs. Scarlett Jordan..

Keep waiting till that..

Love y'all

04/04/2018

Chapter 20

Scarlett's POV

When we reached the stage, Eros came forward and put his hand in front of me. Richie left my arm with a kiss on my cheek and with not forgetting to give Eros a nod.

It's show time.

I nervously put my hand in Eros's hand and climbed up the stage.

"You look gorgeous" he said with a smile.

I blushed, but was still nervous about what was going to happen.

Eros didn't forget to give my hand a squeeze of assurance.

We both were standing hand in hand in front of the priest. He was still staring me with an intense gaze.

I was getting nervous with all the gazes and mostly because of Eros gaze.

The Priest started to tell us our vows which we both repeated after him.

"Do you Mr. Eros Jordan accept Ms. Scarlett Miller as your lawfully wedded wife and to cherish her and love her with all your heart?" The priest asked Eros.

Eros looked into my eyes then said "I do".

Everyone in the crowd hooted and clapped for him.

"Do you Ms. Scarlett Miller accept Mr. Eros Jordan as your lawfully wedded husband and to cherish him and love him with all your heart?" The priest asked me this time.

Its the time now.. no going back.. you have to do this for you mom.

I took a deep breath..

"I do" I nervously said.

This time crowd hooted and clapped for me.

"You both may now exchange the rings" the priest said.

We both exchanged the rings.

"I now announce you both lawfully wedded husband and wife. You may kiss the bride" The priest said.

Eros removed the veil from my face and moved his face forward.

"Finally, Mrs. Jordan" he said with a smile.

And touched my lips with his.

Sparks ignited throughout my body.

We both pulled away when the crowd cheered and clapped for both of us. Everyone was so happy and cheery, I can't help but smile at them.

Because they're not the one who's going to live with Mr. Rude.

And with that my smile flew away.

Eros slid his hand on my waist and showed his dimply smile to everyone.

I hope I took right decision to marry him and everything goes well.

-----****-----

We both were seated on the chairs which are alloted for us.

"You are looking so gorgeous today Mrs. Eros Jordan" he teased.

I rolled my eyes.

"Thank you Mr. Jordan" I smiled.

Suddenly he took a hold of my hand in a tight grip.

"Now you are my lawfully wedded wife, so what do you think we should do after the party?" He seductively said.

What is going in his mind?

I blushed at his tone.

I tried to release my hand from his deadly grip but he was too strong.

I stomped on his foot which made him let go of my hand.

I gave him a victorious smirk.

He thinks only he can smirk.

Soon the time for cake cutting came, we both got up from our seats and reached near the cake and where everyone was patiently waiting for us.

Deep down they're like hungry predators.

Right.

The cake was so beautifuly decorated with flowers and a wedded couple standing on the top.

When outerlook of this cake is beautiful, it would be so delicious from inside. Mmm... I can't wait.

I hold the knife with my hand and Eros held the my hand. Tingling sensations run through me by his single touch.

I looked at him and he was already looking at me. So I quickly turned my face away.

Is he also feeling the same?

May be.

We both cut the cake and the crowd applauded loudly.

Hungry peeps

He took a spoonfull of cake and put it front of my mouth. I ate the cake. The cake was actually so yummy. I was about to moan but stopped when I saw him licking the same spoon from which I ate.

Isn't it yuck moment?

I blushed and he moaned.

And my blush deepened.

He came closer to my ear. I can feel his hot breath on my shoulder which caused me to shiver.

"Now it tastes much more delicious when my wife had already tasted it" he said which allowed goosebumps to rose all over my body.

I looked down and tried to hide my blush which made him chuckle.

Soon we both were seated on our places.

"You're so lucky to have an extra hot, extra sexy and extraordinary husband like me, right Scar baby?" He teased.

I was about to reply him but Nick came and interrupted my comeback.

"Shortcake? You didn't listened to me, you chose this idiot over me. What does he has that I dont? I know he's hot but so am I. Where did I go wrong?" he fake cried by rubbing his hands under his eyes.

Aww, he knows how to make a girl smile.

"I'm so sorry Nick, you should have met me before him, I would have surely married you rather than this idiot" I teased back.

Eros narrowed his eyes at me and put his hand on my thigh.

My eyes widened. And a devilish smirk forms on his face.

"My bad, but don't worry. When you'll leave him you can come to me. I'm always available for you, shortcake" he said with a wink.

Eros's grip tightens on my thigh. Goosebumps rose all over my body.

I was not able to gather words because of his hand which was moving up and down making me feel sparks.

"Oh shut up Nick, she won't be leaving me, ever. Right wifey?" he said with a press on my thigh.

I audibly gulped and nodded as no words came from my mouth.

"I know she's trapped by an idiot, she can't do anything now. What's done is done. Anyways congratulations both for your wedding" Nick said with a grin.

"Thank you so much Nick" I smiled at him.

I slapped Eros's hand away but he kept it back on my thigh with a squeeze.

I groaned.

"Hey what are you both doing? Why don't you both dance? It's your wedding, right. You should be the first couple to dance because I really want to dance with some hotties here" Sonya said.

I narrowed my eyes at her.

She just shrugged.

"Baby, she's right let's dance. It's our wedding party and we should dance" Eros said while getting up.

I rolled my eyes and got up.

We reached the center, soon my favourite track started playing. (A/N guys you can imagine whichever songs you want. Its up to you)

I smile came on my face due to the track. Now I really want to dance.

Eros put his hands on my waist and pulled me towards him. My heartbeat quickens due to our proximity. I put both my hands on his tight chest and created some gap between us.

Mmmm, What would his body look like underneath his shirt?

I blushed at the thought.

"You look beautiful when you blush my dear wifey, but I really wanna know what thoughts are going in your mind" he teased.

Which makes my blush go deeper.

We danced for don't know how much long but when we stopped the crowd was cheering and clapping for us.

Soon it's the time to wrap up the party.

Now I have to throw the flower bouquet to the girls.

Sonya was glaring at me or like warning me that if I didn't threw it at her, she's going to kill me for sure.

Isn't she so desperate?

I think the same.

I turned around and threw the bouquet back.

I heard gasps.

What did you do?

Did you break someone's face or something?

But they were just flowers.

But they were the flowers thrown by you.

When I turned around the bouquet was in Nick's hand.

What?

Seriously?

I can't control my laugh at the scene. He has an innocent expression on his face.

Poor Nick, now he have to face all the girl's wrath. I'll pray for him.

Soon me and Eros left the party and headed towards his home after an emotional farewell with my mom and friends. And unexpectedly Richie cried his heart out. He was looking cute when he cried like a baby. He was sobbing so badly, I think he's the only one who was crying that bad.

When we reached his home I take a look at his house, but it was not any house. It was a mansion, a very beautiful mansion.

I looked at Eros he smiled at me.

"I hope you like your new home " he said.

Eros hold my hand and took me towards the entrance. He opened the door by punching some code.

As I was about to enter but I felt myself lift off from the floor.

Eros lifted me and look at him in shock.

"Can't help, rituals" he said innocently.

Wow! Ain't he so sweet.

I rolled my eyes but on inside I was doing a happy dance at his gesture.

He made me stand in the middle of his house, I looked around in aww.

Wow! Am I dreaming? Are you seriously going to live here.

The mansion is more beautiful from inside as from outside.

The mansion was coloured in grey colour, in the center was a black coloured sofa. I can see the kitchen which is on the right side and from the left side the stairs were going up.

"Your house is so beautiful" I told him.

"Honey it's ours now" he winked.

Aww! Our huh?

I blushed.

"Do you want to see our bedroom?" He asked by coming closer to me.

"Um, y-yeah.. s-sure"

Why the hell I'm stuttering?

Because you are stupid.

What an answer.

"This way, do you wanna walk or want me to lift you up? I won't mind lifting you" he teased and walked towards me.

"N-no.. I'll walk" I said by stepping backwards.

He chuckled and shook his head.

He turned around and started walking towards the stairs. I hesitantly followed him.

Soon we entered a large room having a king size bed, with beige coloured walls, a brown coloured sofa on the right, a dressing mirror near it and two doors both in the opposite direction.

Amazing.

"The door on the left is for washroom, make yourself comfortable. I'll be back in a few minutes" he said as he left the room.

I sighed.

Let's be free and get relieved from this killer dress. I can't breathe properly in it. It was too heavy.

Yeah you must have gained wait after eating like an animal in the party.

I didn't eat that much.

I can only see you in the whole party stuffing your mouth.

Shut up.

I sat in front of the dressing mirror and wiped off the makeup from my face. I removed all the accesories from my hairs as they were making my pain in my head.

I tried to open the zipper of my dress but I was not able to reach it. Stupid zipper.

How did I wore it?

With the help of the stylists, duh.

Right.

After a lot of attempt I gave up.

I'll ask for someone's help.

I sighed.

Suddenly their was knock on the door and Eros came in with a velvet box in his hand.

What's in the box?

I instantly got up.

He came near me and gave the box to me.

"What's this?" I questioned.

"This is your wedding gift from your hot and sexy husband, my dear wifey" he grinned.

"What is in it?" I again asked.

"Why don't you see it by yourself?" He said.

I confusingly took it and open its lid. My eyes widens at the thing in the box.

The box contains a very beautiful pendant. Its silver in colour and diamonds are embedded into it. It was very cute. I took it out and gazed towards its beauty. Then I look towards Eros he was staring at me with a dazzling smile.

This is so beautiful.

"May I?" He asked.

I nodded.

He took it from me and turned me around and tied it.

I looked in the mirror, it looks perfect on me.

"I personally requested to make this, it is one of its kind, it suits you. Do you like it?" he asked by kissing the back of my neck.

I blushed and nodded.

"Thank you so much, I really loved it, it's really very beautiful, you don't have to bring this "I replied while touching the necklace.

"You were really looking so beautiful today" he said.

"And not to forget, you didn't bumped into me today" he teased.

Yeah, that's a new thing.

I blushed and covered me face with my hands.

He laughed at my action.

"You're seriously so cute wifey " he teased.

Did he forget about yesterday's night?

I wish he did.

How am I going to survive with him?

Hello lovely readers..

Finally Mr. Rude made Scarlett his Mrs. Rude..

What will happen in future..

Will they make peace or will rip each other's head off..

To know.. keep on reading..

Love y'all

05/05/2018

Chapter 21

Eros's POV for all of you guys

You all wants to know , right? What's going on his mind?

Enjoy

Eros's POV

Days went on a great speed and day after tomorrow I'll be getting married to my Scarlett.

A totally whipped man talks.

I rolled my eyes.

Since the day of engagement party when I kissed her. I want to touch her, feel her, pamper her and I really can't wait to spend my rest of life with her. Everyday I think about her all the time. I want her to be mine as soon as possible.

Now whipped plus possessive man talks.

Shut up.

She will be mine in two days. I can't wait that to happen. Scarlett, What are you doing to me?

I was getting ready for my bachelor's party where Nick is forcefully dragging me to live my life little before getting married.

It was before meeting Scarlett that I want a girl to hangout with but now there's only her, now I always think about spending my time with her. I have to go as Nick emotionally blackmailed me by showing his drama from which I can't slip away.

So here I'm getting ready for the last party of my bachelor self. I am wearing a white T and beige coloured pants, a black blazer and I completed my look with white sneakers. I sprayed my cologne, finally I'm ready to go to that stupid party. Hope it wouldn't be a disaster.

My room's door burst open and Nick came in and glanced me up to down.

"Why? Why do you always look better than me" he huffed by crossing his hands over his chest.

I chuckled.

"Because I'm better than you"I shrugged.

"Yeah yeah why not, so are you ready to go?" He asked.

"Is it necessary for me to go. I don't wanna go" I said.

And there will be no Scarlett.

Exactly.

"Are you insane? It's your bachelor's party and you're saying you don't wanna go. After tomorrow you'll be no more bachelor, you will be a married man. Oh my dear friend, I feel bad for you" he fake cried.

"You're overreacting " I stated.

"Am I?" He questioned.

I nodded.

"You won't understand what it feels like when your best friend is getting married" he dramatically said.

"Nick" I groaned.

"Okay, I'll stop. Now let's get moving" he said.

With that we both left my room. We were going to my club to celebrate my last happy days.

What would Scarlett be doing? I can't help but think about her.

She would be speaking or more like screaming with her speaker self.

May be.

We reached the club and parked our car and entered the club and reached to the VIP lounge, a few girls were staring and seductively showing me with their fake body assets but I just ignored them and carried on my way to the lounge. We got seated and ordered our drinks.

A slutty waitress came and bend while showing me a great view of cleavage, but I showed no interest which I think she doesn't understood and keep on showing her cleavage.

Nick was watching me with an amused look. I know he is enjoying this.

"Don't you see I'm not at all interested in your cleavage. Do you even know who am I? If you won't stop this I will fire you. Now go away" I scolded her.

The waitress hurriedly walked away or more like ran away. Nick bursted out laughing at the scene. I showed him the deadliest glare I can gather.

"Poor girl" he amusingly said.

I huffed in annoyance.

"Come on man, don't show me that face. She's gone and must be crying in a corner. You frightened her. Now forget about it and enjoy" he said and raised his glass for a toast.

I shook my head and raised my glass to him. We clinked the glass and I gulped down the liquid in one go. Nick soon refilled my glass. As I was taking a sip I can't help but to think about Scarlett, what she would be doing right now.

"What do you think Scarlett would be doing?" I asked Nick out of curiosity.

"Aww, my friend is totally whipped. He's missing his soon to be wedded wife. Now I'm jealous" he teased.

I narrowed my eyes at him.

"Okay okay. Don't scare me, about Scarlett, according to me she would be partying hard in a club where she was enjoying while she'd be surrounded by a lots of men" he said.

Lots of men? What?

"What are you saying? Why would she be enjoying with lots of men?" I questioned.

"These are the usual things that happens in a bachelorett's party"he stated.

"I don't think this would happen, Scarlett is not that kind of girl" I said or more like asking myself.

"Bro chillax, yes she's not like that but the things I told you were common in this type of party. Let her enjoy, it's not like she's going to sleep with anyone, she knows she'll marry you, if she was surrounded by male strippers or.." I cut him off.

"Shut up! Do you know where would she be?" I asked.

"Yeah! Don't tell me you're planning something" He questioned by raising an eyebrow.

"Let's give my would be wifey a visit" I said as I gulped down my remaining drink and got up from my seat and went towards the car. I know Nick was hot on my heels. We both drove off to that club.

It's the time to show her whom she belongs.

When we reached the club, I gave my keys to Nick so he can park the car and I'll search for Scarlett. When I entered the club I got blinded by neon lights and the music was on full volume, but I have to search for Scarlett so I checked around and when I found her, my eyes widens.

What is she wearing? Isn't it so short? But damn she looks sexy as hell.

She was in a black dress that makes her look so sexy, she was swaying her hips with the music like nothing else matters to her. I kept on watching her for a few minutes but when our eyes meet she stopped on her spot. Glancing at me without blinking her eyes looking confused.

Without wasting anymore time and ignoring Nick who just entered now I went towards her. When I reached in front of her I grasped her tightly in my arms but she pushed me away.

What the hell happened to her? Why is she pushing you away?

I asked her if she was alright because she is not recognising me. I'm her soon to be husband how can she forget me?

I think she's not Scarlett. Is she her duplicate? Because she's too sexy to be Scarlett.

She replied to me by a grin.

Why is she grinning? Bro I think it's the time.

For what?

To take her to the mental hospital.

I rolled my eyes.

Shut up!

As you wish.

She raised her hand and touched my cheek. Her touch was so soft and smooth, after talking with her for sometime I came to know that she's not recognising me at all. So I took that opportunity to dig deeper, I want to know how does she feels about me? Am I the only one who is facing this thing to be close to her, thinking about her all time, always want to be near her?

Does she also feels the same?

So I started asking her questions about her, is she happy with the wedding, I don't want to force her but what can I do, I really want her.

My heart crumpled down when I asked her if she wants to marry me and why is she marrying me and she told me that it was all for her mom and my mom's bond. I really felt bad at that time, but my hopes got high when she said she's somehow attracted to me not as much as me but it's a progress, right, and somewhere she founds me hot, sexy as well as handsome. I'm so happy right now and the way she was laughing and giggling, I found myself getting more attracted to her. She's so cute so innocent.. and you're so whipped.

Shut up! Don't spoil the mood.

After talking for a while she dragged me to get seated and she ordered a drink for her. As she was sipping her drink I kept on staring at her, she's looking hot in that dress and her drunken state makes her cute. In her drunken state she kept on praising me, and every compliment from her mouth for me makes my heart go wild. She's so beautiful. She was rambling every thought that she have in her mind for me without a thought. She was that drunk.

But when she mentioned our first kiss, heat flowed through my body by only thinking about her soft lips on mine, and most importantly she enjoyed it as much as I did and she also thinks I'm a pro. I was literally on seventh heaven now, after knowing her thoughts about me. God! I'm so lucky to have her in my life.

And I'm really happy a 24/7 entertainer would always be at home with us.

After few minutes of her rambling she went quiet for a while and when I thoroughly checked her and she was gripping her seat tightly and her eyes were closed. I asked her if she was alright, she told me she's feeling dizzy. So I suggested that we should go home which she unexpectedly obliged. I paid the bill of her drink and helped her to get up but she was not able to stand so I hold her by her shoulder to give her support and we walked towards the exit.

I turned around before exiting the car and looked for Nick and when I found her I action him that I'm leaving with Scarlett and Nick being Nick made some kissing actions by the tips of hands and making a pouty face. I glared at him and left the club towards my car.

I took her to my car and made her seated and walked across the car and sat in my seat. She was still not recognising me. How can she be that drunk? I don't take her for a drunkard type. I don't know how is she this drunk?

She keeps on telling me that I look like Eros and I also smell like him and she founds my cologne intoxicating the whole ride. A goofy smile was on my face the whole ride. I'm really liking this side of Scarlett. When we reached her home I exited my car and I opened her side of door and asked her if she was able to walk. She said that she can but when she stepped out of the car her steps faltered and I caught her just in time.

She was so drunk and was not able to walk so I swiftly carried her in my arms and walked towards her home. She was so close to me, I can see that she was staring at me which is not making this situation any helpful. I knocked the door to her house and her mom opened the door but she didn't asked anything and stepped aside with a deadly smile.

I walked inside and carried her to her room and laid her down on her bed and sat beside her with her hands in mine. She was staring me without blinking her eyes. She is too cute when she's drunk.

And gets more stupid.

A stupid smile was still present on my face.

"You look very cute when you are drunk "I said by touching her body with my fingers.

I came closer and was looking her face. I can see her face, she's so beautiful just like an angel with such innocence. But what surprised me the most she asked me if she can kiss me, like really kiss me. And who am I to say no to her. I greedily obliged and placed my lips on hers. Our lips molded with each others. Our lips were moving in a sync. My one hand was on her cheek and other was balancing me. But soon I pulled away as I don't want to take her advantage when she's not stable and she can't even recognise me.

She's never stable.

I stood up and placed a firm kiss on her forehead and was about to go when she grabbed my hand and stopped me from going by calling me by my name in mere whisper. Her whisper erupted shiver in my body. I slowly turned around her and the way she said me to stay with her, i was ready to oblige but I can't do that right. We are soon getting married and I can't stay here when she's drunk. But I can stay till she sleeps, right? So I sat beside her with a smile and laid her down on the bed. She was holding my hand so tightly like her life depends on it. I smiled at her cute gesture. I kissed her forehead and wished her good night. I lied beside her and tightly hugged her. Her fragrance was intoxicating even she's drunk. I buried my face in her neck and inhaled deeply.

At last she recognises you, pheww.

"We both have a big day after tomorrow, sleep tight baby" I said.

"Then you'll be only mine " I stated

Soon I started hearing her stable breathes means she was asleep. I pecked her lips once more before leaving and wrote a note on a paper as I know she'll surely forget about today's events by tomorrow. After writing I left her home and drove towards mine.

After tomorrow you'll be mine Scarlett.

Hello guys..

Did you missed Eros?

Want more POV's?

Thank you all for reading

I hope you like the chapter

Keep on commenting and voting

Love you all

06/04/2018

Chapter 22

E ros's POV

Kiss me Eros, please. I want you to kiss me please. I want your lips on mine. Please Eros, please.

Really? She wants me to kiss her, and who am I to say no to her. I'll definitely kiss her soft lips.

I held my Scar firmly by her shoulders and slowly pulled her forward towards me,

She closed her eyes and was waiting for my lips to get attached to her.

I looked at her pink plump kissable lips, begging me to kiss them. I slowly moved forward towards her, vanishing the distance between us.

I am so close to her.

I can feel her breath on my face.

I was so close to feel her lips on mine.

So close to make her lips touch mine.

So close,

Suddenly,

I heard a scream.

My eyes jerk open and the view in front of me was not good.

It's worst.

I was holding Nick's shoulders and was about to kiss him.

Can someone please say, Ewww.

"Please leave me for my future wife. I didn't know that you have feelings for me. Leave me please. For the sake of your would be wife "he cried by joining his hands.

Shit! I was holding Nick not Scarlett. Ugh! Thank God I didn't kiss him. How would I have lived with such a memory of me kissing Nick?

Cringy.

I pushed Nick away from me and took a deep breath still thanking God that he didn't let that happen.But I can still see Nick giving me weird expression.

"Oh shut up, I didn't do that intentionally, I was sleeping. It's your fault you shouldn't have to be so close to me" I replied by rubbing my eyes.

Yeah, you were dreaming about your Scarlett.

"Right, you are right. It was all my fault now, how rude can you be of accusing your only friend who is so smart and sexy and who is totally straight and was going to be kissed by his bestie. I wanna die, I can't live in this cruel world where a poor man like me can't be safe" he over dramatically said.

Poor Nick. I feel really bad for him,

I rolled my eyes.

"Nick shut all your drama right now, I don't want to talk about it. Let's just forget what was about to happen and tell me what are you doing here at this hour" I asked while getting up from the bed.

"It's not drama bro, you scared me by doing that horrible thing. How would I show my face to others? Oh holy Jesus! what have I done to have a friend like him who was about to kiss me, why would any girl wanna marry me if this really happened " he fake cried.

That's enough.

"Nick" I yelled.

"Forget it, You won't understand my feelings" he said by standing up from my bed.

"Anyways, I came hear as my bro you have your wedding to attend and it's half past 11. You should start getting ready now, we don't want to be late, do we?"he said by folding his sleeves.

Damn!

I too forgot about the wedding, your friend is a tremendous actor, he literally made me hate you.

I rolled my eyes.

"I seriously forgot about the wedding just because your drama" I told him.

He just shrugged.

"Your tux has arrived and every thing is in the room, hurry up now, get yourselves ready" he said by clapping his hands. He then left my room and

I went to the bathroom and took a nice shower. I came out and wore my tux, which has white shirt and blue pants and a blue blazer, with a tie, I gelled my hair back and sprayed my favorite cologne.

I glanced at the mirror and checked for any defect, when I didn't find any I exited my room and headed downstairs. When I reached downstairs my mom, Anna and Nick were looking at me constantly making that scene creepy..

Are you looking like a joker? Why are they staring at you like that?

I walked towards them and stood in front of them, they still were not blinking their eyes. They were still staring at me. I cleared my throat to break their trance. I think my mom first came out of her trance because she started blinking her eyes rapidly and burst into tears. I moved forward and hugged her tightly.

Aww, such a lovely moment.

"My son is getting married today. I can't believe that it's actually happening. You were so small and now look you are not a boy but a man and you're getting married today. You look so handsome. I'm very happy to see you like this" she said by tightly embracing me. Anna came forward and hugged us both,

"I'm so happy for you brother, you found your perfect match. You both look awesome together. I wish you both live happily in future" Anna said.

I hugged her then kissed her forehead, then my mom's and smiled at both.

Soon I heard someone's sniffing sound.

Who can it be? You have comforted your mom and Anna is in front of you, then, who's the one crying now?

I looked towards my right.

And there I found the one crying.

Nick,

He was flowing waterfall from his eyes. He was trying to control himself but miserably failing in it.

I moved towards him and hugged him. And patted his back to soothe him.

Then he started crying out loudly.

You sure, right? That you're getting married not leaving them?

"My bestie is getting married today. I can't believe it, you're looking so smart and handsome as always, my only friend. Please don't forget me after getting married, I'm you're only friend right " he said by tightly embracing me in a bone crushing hug.

He's so nice friend. Always there to help you.

I smiled at Nick. Sometimes he can be such a baby.

"No Nick I'm not going to forget you even if I try and yes you'll be my only friend" I said by rubbing his back.

"I love you bro" he said.

I love him too.

"Shall we leave now for the venue? I don't wanna be late" I questioned.

"Someone's getting restless to see his bride" Mom teased.

I just shrugged.

In real I want to see her, her single smile can make my heart go insane.

What is she? A clown?

I ignored my inner voice.

Soon we left for the venue. When we reached the venue I was so happy that everything is according to Scar's wish as Sonya told me. The venue was looking so beautiful with white surroundings. I can't wait to see Scarlett.

I walked towards the alter and waited there for my would-be wife to arrive.

Have patience, she'll be here soon.

After few minutes of tapping my foot and counting all the chairs, the music finally started playing which means she's here. And it's my cue to look at the entrance.

Here comes the bumping girl of your dreams.

An alluring looking Scarlett was walking down the aisle towards me, slowly slowly, she was looking down but as she felt my gaze on her she glanced at my side, I smiled at her.

I can see that she's so damn nervous.

She's looking so beautiful like an angel walking towards me, in a white gown and in a long veil holding a bouquet of flowers and the main thing is that this angel is walking down the aisle for me. She's going to be my angel, my Scarlett, my wife.

She was walking with Richie by her side. Soon they came towards the alter, I walked forward and gave her my hand.

Richie kissed her forehead and nodded towards me and left with a smile.

"You look gorgeous" I told her with a smile.

She nodded, she was looking innocent I was totally mesmerized by the way she was looking at me. Her eyes were sparkling. I took her hand and we walked to the center facing each other, hand in hand in front of the priest.

But I can see it in her eyes that she is so nervous, so I squeezed her hand to assure her that I'm with her, for her, always.

And when she smiled at me, I was literally floating in heaven. Her looks got completed with her sweet and simple smile. I was gawking at her totally forgetting where am I standing, who was watching me and what is going on.

My main focus is on my Scarlett, I kept watching her little little details of her face, her blue eyes filled with nervousness, shining because of the daylight. I can see her face whole day. Never thought I will be in a position where nothing will matter to me except one girl.

I got interrupted when the priest called my name and told me that's its time to take the vows and after taking the vows it's finally time to make her my wife. So the priest asked me that if I take her as my lawfully wedded wife, the time for which I was waiting for don't know how much time came. After this she'll be my wife, my life.

I took a deep breath before saying "I do". A chorus of cheering and shouting erupted from the guests. After hearing my acceptance the priest asked the same question to Scarlett that she accepts me as her husband. She took a deep breath and took her time to reply "I do", I released my breath which don't know I was holding.

The priest announced us both as a husband wife and it's to seal it with a kiss. A slow smile crept on my face on thinking about that Scarlett's my wife now. Mrs. Jordan. I brought my face forward towards her so that I can kiss her. Her eyes gets closed instantly, I came closer to her and captured her lips in a sealing kiss. At that time nothing mattered to me, only thing matters to me was my wife, my Scarlett.

Congrats ..you finally got her.

We both pulled away when the crowd cheered and clapped for both of us. We walked further towards the crowd and I know I'm grinning like a fool, but in my defense you don't get married everyday. I slid my arm on her waist and when she didn't make any effort to get herself out of grip, I was so happy. At least she accepts me as her husband.

Scarlett is finally mine and only mine.

I kept a firm hold of her hand as I was not in a mood to leave her, so we left for the after wedding party hand in hand. A goofy smile was still present on my face.

_____****_____

We both were now seated on the chairs which are allotted for us and I was still looking at her. How can someone be so beautiful and most importantly this beauty is my wife now.

Yeah she's beautiful from face but too damn stupid from mind. How can someone be so stupid?

But she's cute too.

"You are looking ravishing today Mrs. Eros Jordan" I teased and I can see pink colour crept towards her cheeks. She cleared her throat before replying me.

"Thank you Mr. Jordan" she smiled a little bit.

I had an urge to hold her hand so I did it and hold her soft hand in mine.

"Now you are my lawfully wedded wife, so what do you think we should do after the party?" I seductively said.

Staring at her now widen eyes and a dark pink colour appears on her face. She was trying hard to remove her hand from mine but she's not getting success. I won't leave this hand ever. But she did something unexpected, she stomped on my foot which made me groan.

Fiesty much.

With which she released her hand from my grip.

Now you saved yourself from me but for how long Scarlett. You can't run away form me. Afterall we are going to live together.

I smirked at the thought.

You have to accept me soon, I'll make sure of that,

My Scarlett.

Chapter completed..

Hurray

I hope you all like it.

Keep reading and supporting.

Love you guys

Chapter 23

E ros's POV

It's the time to cut the cake, I helped her to get up and we both reached near the cake and everyone was clapping and cheering for us.

She hold the knife with her hand then looked towards me, telling me to join her. So I hold her hand instead of holding the knife. She shuddered under my touch. An unknown sensation ran through me.

I looked at her.

She also looked at me. But she quickly turned her face away.

Does she felt the same?

May be, but I hope she does.

We both cut the cake and the crowd applauded loudly.

I took a spoonfull of cake and put it front of her mouth. She ate the cake and smiled at me.

I licked the same spoon from which she ate. It's delicious now.

She blushed and I moaned in the delicious taste.

She gulped which formed a smirk on my face.

I came closer to her ear.

"Now it tastes so delicious when my wife had already tasted it" I said.

I can see the goosebumps that rose all over her body due to our closeness.

She immediately looked down and tried to hide her blush.

She looked so cute at this moment.

I chuckled at her state.

Soon we both were attended the guests. After attending a few guests, we both once again were back to our places. I can't help but want to tease her so I teased her.

"You're so lucky to have an extra hot, extra sexy and extraordinary husband like me, right Scar baby?" I teased.

I just love teasing her.

She was glaring at me but Nick interrupted her.

Why Nick why? We were having fun.

Nick came and started flirting with her. A feel of jealousy ran throughout me. I know Nick is my friend and he don't see Scar in that way but I can't help myself, this jealousy is making me feel stupid things. I gathered my most deadliest glare and shot it towards him, but Nick being Nick, he ignored all my daggers and kept flirting with my wife.

What is he saying? He knows that you are head over heels for her. He knows that you're totally whipped.

Shut up. I'm not whipped.

Yeah! I'm whipped right?

It was not enough that Nick was flirting with her that Scar also started to flirt back with him. I'm getting annoyed by their flirting.

Now this is enough, if I can't stop Nick I surely can stop her, Right?

I narrowed my eyes at her. She should have known that by now that she's mine and only mine. No sharing. She really loves to tease me. So to tease her back,

I put my hand on her thigh and squeezed it a little.

Her eyes widen and her face started turning red.

A smirk forms on my face.

Nick asked her that her if she will leave with him after me and this was the thing that made me angry, so I shouted at him to stop him.

She's not going to leave me for anyone, not now not ever. She'll be mine forever.

Aaha! Possessive much.

"Oh shut up Nick, she won't be leaving me.. ever, right my dear wifey?" I said with a press on her thigh. I can see her eyes widen and how she gulped. It's great to know that my touch effects her. She nodded in Nick's direction telling him that I was right, she's not going to leave me. I grinned to myself at that thought.

But here the person who is openly flirting to my wife was Nick, and he don't know the meaning of no. He continued flirting with her knowing that there is no chance for him.

He really likes to annoy me and he very well know I'm totally annoyed with him. So to shut him up I shot him my deadliest glare and mouthed "You are dead", this made him stop flirting, he audibly gulped so he congratulated us and was off in no time.

Due to my concentration on shooing Nick away I forgot about where my hand is placed, which is now not on Scar's thigh because she slapped my hand away, and me being the most stubborn guy I put it back on her thigh with a squeeze telling her that I'm not moving my hand now. She was not expecting that squeeze, she jumped on her place and shot daggers towards me, and I was smiling like a fool on her jumping. When I was about to make a snarky comment, Sonya disturbed me.

"Hey what are you both doing why don't dance? As it's your wedding, you should be the first couple to dance. Now hurry up. Everyone's waiting " Sonya said.

Yeah, Let's break the floor..I like the girl Sonya, she always helps us.

"Baby, she's right let's dance. It's our wedding party and our dancing is must, right? Now shall we?" I said while getting up and giving her my hand,

She rolled her eyes but obliged and got up from her seat and placed her hand in mine. When we reached the center, a romantic track started playing. A cute smile appeared on her face. She was looking so angelic with her small smile.

Bro, you are totally whipped.

I placed my hands on her waist and pulled her towards me, she was so close to me, she puts both her hands on my chest, I melt under her touch. I can feel the heat of her hands beneath my shirt. She turned her gaze towards the floor because of which I was not able to see her eyes, so I placed my finger under her chin and pushed it upward so can I see her eyes, she somehow got my message and looked straight into my eyes. I can clearly see the pink appearing on her cheeks. She's blushing,

She looks so stunning with her pink cheeks. My hands are itching to touch her now pink cheeks.

"You look beautiful when you blush dear wifey " I teased.

Which makes her cheeks turn into dark pink. She didn't replied so I also kept quiet and enjoyed the moment with Scarlett in my arms. We danced for don't know how much time but when we stopped the crowd was cheering and clapping for us.

She lowered her gaze due to embarrassment, so I gave her a comforting side hug. She visibly relaxed.

Soon it's the time to wrap up the party.

I left Scarlett to complete her further rituals.

I met a few important people to see them off.

Suddenly I heard someone's laughter, when I turned around I see Scarlett laughing.

A slow smile came to my face. When I looked towards the way she was laughing which made a smile crack on my face. She looked so carefree, but when I searched for their reason for laughing,

Nick was holding the bouquet that should be in a girl's hand.

All the girls were accusing him for this.

He has an innocent expression on his face.

Poor Nick. I feel bad for him.

Soon we both bid our goodbyes to everyone and left the venue and head towards my.. oh sorry.. our home.

I smiled at the thought of our home. We'll both live together.

Yeah, before now you were living with the ghosts and devils, like your mum and now you'll be living with a speaker. Sorry, stupid speaker.

I rolled my eyes.

When we reached our home she looked at house with wide eyes.

Don't she like the house?

Relax bro she is stupid but not this much to not like a mansion.

After few minutes she glanced at me.

In reply I smiled at her.

"I hope you like your new home " I said.

I took a hold of her hand and walked with her towards the entrance.

I punched the codes and opened the door.

Hey bro you remember no? The devil.. um, I mean your mom told you about the rituals after the marriage. Please don't forget them, otherwise your mom will make Eros name forget from the world.

I totally forgot about it, thanks for reminding me.

Anytime, I want myself to be safe. I don't wanna see your mom's devil side. Now be a good husband and do the rituals nicely.

I nodded.

I turned towards her and lift her off the floor in my arms.

She's too light weight.

So? Do you want a light weight bride or a bouncer.

Oh Shut up.

She was purely shocked because I lift her off without informing her. She squealed and started wriggling in my arms, I tightened my hold on her.

"Can't help.. rituals" I told her.

She rolled her eyes but didn't make any further movement.

I made her stand in the middle and searched for any staff available or not.

She was glancing the house in aww, her expressions look like she was amazed to look at the house interiors.

She was looking at the house and I was looking at her.

After a few minutes she spoke,

"Your house is beautiful" She told me.

"Honey it's ours now" I winked.

She blushed.

"Do you want to see our bedroom?" I asked by coming closer to her.

Her face turned red like a tomato. I controlled my laugh,

"Um.. y-yeah.. s-sure"She stuttered.

She get's nervous because of me.

Victooorrryyyyy.

"This way, by the way, do you wanna walk or want me to lift you up" I teased.

She blushed but shook her head.

"N-no.. I'll walk"She said.

I can't help but to chuckle at her nervousness.I started walking towards the stairs by glancing back at her time to time. When we entered our room, Our bedroom.

She was looking at the whole room in aww.

She was looking at the doors so I told her about the doors.

"The door on the left is for washroom, make yourself comfortable. I'll be back in a few minutes" I said as I left the room.

I have to give her the wedding gift which was customized on my demand.

It was a very cute pendant which I found perfect for her soft neck.

Control man control your thoughts.

I kept it in my office as I didn't found any more safer place to keep it and I want it to be nearby me, I hurriedly walked towards my office and opened the locker and removed the velvet box from it.

I ran towards the room as I don't wanna be away from her when she is already in my room

I opened my room's door and found her sitting in front of the dressing mirror.

Now she looks even more beautiful without any layer of make up, her hairs were down from the bun. She's a real beauty.

She first looked at me then at my hands. She stood up from her seat and turned towards me.

I walked towards her stand in front of her, and gave her the box which is in my hands.

"What's this?" She questioned confusingly.

"This is your wedding gift my dear wifey" I smiled at her.

"What is in it?" She again asked.

She's so restless.

"Why don't you see it by yourself?" I told her.

I stared at her with a smile as she was glancing the pendant. I hope she liked it.

"May I?" I asked.

She nodded.

I took it out from the box and turned her around and tied it to her neck.

"I personally requested to make this, it is one of its kind, it suits you. Do you like it?" I asked by kissing the back of her neck.

She blushed.

"Thank you so much, I really loved it, it's really very beautiful, you don't have to bring this "She replied while touching the pendant.

"You were really looking so gorgeous today" I told her and slid my hands on her waist and pulled her closer towards me. I can feel her soft body against me.

"And not to forget, you didn't bumped into me today" I teased.

She embarrassingly lowered her gaze and covered her face with her hands.

She looks cute doing that.

I laughed.

"You're seriously so cute wifey " I teased.

She'll be the death of me, but I'm happy she's mine, my wife, it's like a missing puzzle of my life placed in the right place.

All because of my dear Scarlett.

/speaker.

Pheww...

Finally completed..

Chapters are getting longer day by day..

But for you it's nothing..

Keep on voting and supporting..

Love y'all

08/04/2018

Chapter 24

Eros

Scarlett's POV

I was standing in his room debating whether I should ask help from him or should wait till morning?

Listen stop being stupid and ask for his help. Because I need my beauty sleep.

Okay.

"Um.. Eros.. I need a favour from you. Can you please pull the zipper of my dress down? I'm not able to reach it, as you know I have to sleep and in this dress I can't sleep it's so huge and so difficult to manage, if you-" I rambled on but Eros cut me off in the mid,

"Scarlett, I'll do it" he replied with a tight smile. He slowly slowly undid the zipper, my breath hitched, I can feel the heat radiating from his hands. My heart started beating madly, I think it forgot it's rhythm as his fingers touched my bare back, my whole body shivered under his touch.

When I look at his reflection in the mirror he was already looking at me, without blinking. The intensity of his stare made me look down on the floor, I audibly gulped.

Soon I felt him tracing his fingers on my bare back, his calloused hands against my skin. It erupted unknown feelings in my body. I was not able to look at him in the mirror because I know his eyes would be on mine. He came more closer, his breath fanned the crook of my neck, goosebumps rose all over my body. Then I felt something soft pressed against the crook of my neck,

I immediately glanced up in the mirror, his lips were on my neck, peppering it with kisses. I melted under his touch, I think my body organs must be partying inside.

He showered kisses on the back of my neck and continued this torture till he reached my back. I was totally under his mercy. I can feel butterflies having fun inside my stomach. His kisses were doing some kind of magic on me, which I never wanted to stop.

Slowly he turned me around and caressed my cheeks with the back of his palm. I think the shade of his eyes turned a shade darker, and the most awaited thing happened, he kissed me on my lips,

His lips were molded to mine

Fireworks burst through out me, my body was on fire.

Our lips were moving in perfect sync, he deepens the kiss and grabbed my waist tightly and my hands on its accord reach towards his soft and silky hairs pulling him more towards me,

Soon oxygen demanded its entrance and we pulled apart or more like I pulled back because he was now assaulting my neck with his kisses,

He was showering kisses on my neck, he slowly moved his lips to my shoulder, his soft lips on me, I was drowning in that feel.

Our moment was interrupted by a knock at the door.

We both abruptly pulled away panting, I know I must be red by now, Eros cleared his throat but his voice was still husky,

"I think your bag of clothes are here, um.. I should get them" he said by scratching the back of his neck.

Then he walked towards the door, opened it and brought my bags in.

"Mm.. you can change here. I will use the other room" he said.

I awkwardly nodded, he took his clothes from the closet and exits the room.

I released my breath which I was holding, and ran towards the door and locked it, making sure that no one enters, I leaned on the door, liking the cool touch of the door,

What just happened? Why can't I stop myself? Why I can't ignore his touch?

Because you are attracted to him,

No, I'm not. How can I be? He's so rude.

I sighed and then removed my dress and wore something comfy and then opened the door's lock.

Where am I going to sleep?

That's a really good question for someone who is standing in a bedroom.

Uhh!! Why are you so annoying?

Because I'm your inner voice.

Shut up.

Suddenly the room's door opens and Eros entered only in sweatpants, nothing on the top, his muscled chest was on full display,

Looking so hot should be banned by the government.

My cheeks turned red at the sight,

He looked towards me and a devilish smirk formed on his face.

"I like your shorts" he winked.

I looked down and looked at the shorts I'm wearing. I'm wearing a sponge-bob shorts which are really short shorts. A blush crept on my face as I noticed his gaze on my legs,

I cleared my throat.

"Why are you not wearing something on your upper side?" I questioned.

I don't mind him if he stay in that only.

Why would you?

"Because wifey I sleep like this" he replied with a shrug.

Sleeping with him when he is half naked, amazing.

"Please wear something" I requested by shifting my gaze from him.

You should also see the live beauty, everyone don't get to see that daily.

"How about no, do you have any problem in looking at my abs? Baby a lot of hard work is done to gets these" he said by actioning towards his abs.

"And you want me to hide them? No chance wifey" He stated with a finality.

He's so full of himself.

I groaned,

"But I can't sleep like that" I whined.

Yeah, I know you won't be able to control yourself.

Shut up. It's not like that.

Babe I know you very well.

"Awe, my wifey can't control herself. How will an innocent person like me will sleep peacefully in this room? When a hungry woman is going to be in the same room" He fake cried by covering his chest with his hands.

Innocent and he? ROFL.

"Shut up" I said.

He chuckled and jumped on the bed.

Is he sleeping here?

May be he'll tell me about some other room to sleep.

"Where am I sleeping?" I asked.

"Here, right beside your sexy husband, I know your'e so excited to sleep right beside me, now come on" he said by patting the place beside him.

What?

"In your dreams" I rolled my eyes and crossed my arms front of my chest,

"You want to sleep with me in dreams too. I didn't know you were that desperate, wifey" he teased.

I blushed red,

"Shut up, I'm not" I groaned.

"Your'e already imagining us sleeping together in your cute little mind, right?" he teasingly said,

" I'm not and I'm not sleeping with you" I huffed.

"You'll sleep on the couch" I told him.

"Nope" he replied.

"Then I'll sleep on it" I said and started walking towards it,

Can you?

"No chance. I don't want that you sprain your neck or something"he stated.

Awe, he cares for you.

"I don't want anyone to accuse me that I was rough with you on our wedding night, I don't want to share our bedtime secret with others" he teased.

I take my words back.

Is he for real?

I stomped my feet on the floor like a child.

"Stop behaving like a child and come sleep here, I won't bite you, till you don't want me to. I can control myself" he winked.

I raised an eyebrow and glared at him.

"No thanks, I'll go and sleep into some other room" I told him.

Bravo!

Scar-1 Eros-0

I grinned.

"Oh no you can't. Those servants are my mom's minions. They'll tell everything about us to mom and I'm in no mood to face my mom, so you have to sleep here only. Right beside me" he seriously said.

I sighed.

Back to zero. I don't think you can beat him.

"Then I'll sleep on the floor" I stated.

"I don't mind you doing so, as long as you don't have any problems with rats? I have seen a few roaming here and there. I think they'll like you. Wanna try?" he asked.

Rats? Oh no no no, please don't sleep on the floor.

I also don't like them.

I left a defeated sigh.

"Okay. I'll sleep on the same bed with you but don't you dare come on my side" I warned him.

"I'll try my best, but I can't guarantee you because my hands automatically reaches towards beauties" he winked.

He called me a beauty, I tried to hide my blush. I walked towards the bed and lied on the farthest corner, away from him.

He chuckled.

"Hey babe I know you're trying hard to ignore my sexy and delicious looks, that's why you are at the farthest corner, let me tell you. You won't be able to ignore me and I'm permanent in your life " he said.

"Don't flatter yourself, you don't look that good, I just don't wanna sleep right next to you" I stated.

Liar. The main reason is you'll end up on him in the morning. You are such a sticky person.

"Is that so? Then what was that when you were saying like I'm so hot and sexy and everyone wants a husband like me, etc. etc.," he said.

What did he just said?

I turned towards him.

"I didn't said anything like that" I told him.

"Oh really?"

Something happened and I found myself buried in the mattress and a very naked chest Eros was hovering over me and gripping my hands above my head in a tight grip, I was not able to move, he's so heavy.

"Last to last night you were saying something about Mr.Rude, like you like him and he's so sexy and hot and not to forget you love his kisses. And not to forget you were requesting him to stay and to kiss you. Do you want me to now? Because I really want to kiss you" he said last line by coming closer to my face.

My eyes widen when he said Mr.Rude.

Shit! He do remember everything. And here I thought he forgot about that.

My eyes widen. I also thought he forgot about that night but no.

Oh my lovely lord why you always make situations like this for me, now what would I reply to him.

I cleared my throat.

"What are you saying?" I acted dumb.

"Acting dumb aren't we?" He questioned.

I groaned and tried to release myself from his deadly grip but nothing happened.

"All that things that I said was being said by the alcohol, I didn't mean a single thing" I boldly stated.

Such a liar.

Deep inside I was praying this moment to end.

"Seriously? Then you won't feel anything when I do this or anything with you" he said.

This? What does he means by this?

What is he gonna to do?

Oh god please save me from the devil.

Not any devil, your devil.

Yippiee..

Finally chapter completed

Thank you everyone for reading, voting, commenting and not too forget your adding this story to your reading list.

Loads of thank you to all.

You all are my spirit to write more and more for you.

Love you guys

09/04/2018

Chapter 25

S carlett's POV

I was thinking what is going on the devil's mind.

His body was still hovering over me, his cologne was making it difficult for me to get away from his grip,

My thoughts got interrupted when he placed his lips on mine.

My body froze as well as my mind. My heart started doing somersault, his lips were working its magic on me, my eyes closes on its accord and soon my lips started moving with his in a sync.

He deepens the kiss and asked for entrance which I surely and obviously refused, I thought he'll leave me but he was having something else on his mind. He took a hold of my hands in his one hand above my head and moved the other along my body touching me, all time his lips attached to mine, because of my wriggling my pj top rose up and exposed a good amount of my stomach and I felt his skin touch with mine,

When I didn't let him dominate the kiss he slid his hand under my pj top. I gasp, because of which he got the opportunity and he did what he wanted to do. His hand was touching my bare stomach, I tried to loosen his grip on my hands but nothing happened.

A moan erupted from somewhere, and I finally notice I was the culprit. Why my body is betraying me?

Soon his kisses traveled down to my neck, I felt helpless as I am hovered by this caveman. Sexy caveman.

I was trying hard to not melt in his touch when he started nibbling my neck and showered pepper kiss.

I groaned but it came like a moan.

I was accusing myself when..oww, I felt a sharp pain on my neck.

He bit me.

My eyes widens.

I pushed him away from me with all the strength I got.

And covered the area of my neck with my hand.

I narrowed my eyes at him.

He grinned like an idiot while staring at me.

Do I look like a clown to him?

I'm not sure about him but for me I'm sure.

"Why did you bit me?" I asked.

"Because I can" he smirked.

"You were lying, when you said that you didn't like my kisses and now, I got my answers dear wifey. How much you don't like my kisses" he winked.

I groaned in response he chuckles, he pecked my lips once again and lied down on his side

I sighed and calmed all my now woken up senses.

"Good night my dear Wifey" he said.

But I ignored him.

I once again reached the farthest corner of the bed and tried to sleep.

When I was half asleep a hand came under my head and turned me around.

A very comfortable pillow came under me and I snuggled to it more because of it's calming heat.

Very familiar and intoxicating fragrance came into my nostrils, I deeply inhaled it.

"You smell so good" I murmured in sleep and I heard a chuckle, I snuggled more to the pillow.

Someone inhaled a deep breath in my neck and kissed my lips then my cheek then my forehead.

"Sleepwell Scarlett " were the last words that I heard before I was off to dreamland.

□□□□

When I woke up I was snuggled into something so comfy, Oh! it must be my pillow. Such a nice pillow I have.

I cuddled more with the pillow when my head collided with a hard chest.

Why do my pillow have a hard chest?

Seriously?

Shit!

I opened my eyes and a peacefully sleeping Eros came into my view, he looks so calm so innocent like he can never be someone related to Mr. Rude.

How can anyone look so beautiful in sleep, so calm so innocent and pure devil when awake.

His one arm was wrapped around me and another was on my waist. Our legs were tangled, I was hovering him.

I blushed at our intimate position,

Everyone looks like a baby as I have read in books but here, he's having that stupid devil's smirk.

I took the opportunity and started noticing every little feature of his face when I heard an husky yet sexy voice.

"It is not good to ogle someone in the early morning dear wifey" he said by tightening his grip around me.

Busted.

I tried to loosen his grip but everything went into vain.

He chuckled at my futile attempts to loosen his grip. I'm feeling embarrassed as I got caught red handed ogling him.

But it's not your fault, he didn't know that you haven't seen someone sexy like him in you whole life.

Why do you always have to insult me?

I didn't say anything wrong, it's hundred percent true.

"Good morning dear wifey" he said with a kiss on my lips.

"G-Good Morning" I stuttered, now why am I stuttering now?

I once again tried to get up but he pulled me back due to which I landed on his bare chest.

I flushed and hide my face in his chest.

He chuckled as his chest vibrated.

"Where are you going my dear wifey? Leaving your extra hot and sexy husband alone in the bed. That's not a good thing." he teased.

He really can't get enough of himself.

I rolled my eyes.

"I'm going to the washroom " I told him.

"Okay wifey, I'm sparing you this time but don't think that every time you'll leave me like this." he once again pecked my lips.

I hurriedly got away from him and was about to fall on my face but he saved me.

Thanks to him, I don't wanna see you kissing the floor early morning.

I ran towards the washroom and locked the door behind me.

I can hear him laughing.

Oh God, where did I put myself into?

After taking a warm and nice bath I decided to leave the bathroom. And being stupid much I forgot to carry my clothes. I know, I know that am I stupid.

But I didn't say anything.

But you're about to.

I peeked through the door by slightly opening it and for my benefit Eros was nowhere to be found.

I hurriedly exited the bathroom and tip toed towards the closet by using my ninja skills and then I bumped into.. you guys know very well,

The one and only,

Eros.

When I gathered my strength and looked up in his green orbs he was staring me with his mouth hung open.

I closed his mouth with my hand. He is so stupid how can someone look at someone so senseless.

But, why is he staring at me?

Stupid, have a look at your self.

But I didn't wore anything wrong... Shit!

Exactly you didn't wore anything wrong.

You're wearing a freaking towel and he's a man.

Please someone kick me and tell me that it is just a dream.

May I do the honors.

He still stood there gawking at me without blinking his eyes.

I did that thing that any one who would be in my situation do.

Are you going to punch him or something?

Nope.

Then you'll kick him. I'm sure.

No way.

Then?

I ran.

I ran as fast as I can towards the bathroom without looking back.

I'm truely speechless.

I heard Eros laughing sound from outside. I face palmed myself.

Shit, shit, shit, why was he there? And why I have to forget my clothes. Ugh! Oh my lovely mother earth please open up and swallow me. I don't want to face him ever again.

And mother earth don't wants you.

After few minutes of roaming around the bathroom I came to know that no one is going to save me from the devil in the room.

As I was planning to exit the room I glanced at the mirror and a red mark was on my neck.

When I touched it, a hickey.

I'm going to kill you Eros.

I groaned by balling my fists in a punch.

I once again exited the bathroom by stomping me feet on the floor.

He glanced at me with raised eyebrow.

"How dare you?" I asked.

"What?" He confusingly asked.

I pointed my finger towards the hickey.

"How can you?" I whined.

He smirked.

"You want a demonstration? Come here. I'll show you" He said.

My eyes widen.

"And as you know you're my wife so I can mark you wherever and whenever I want" he stated.

I groaned, but deep down you're so happy.

I'm not, I took deep breathes to calm my nerves.

"Forget it, would you please leave the room, I need to change" I told him by clutching my towel tightly to me.

"And why would I do that? This is my room and I have no intention to leave my hot wifey who's only in a towel here alone, besides you can change in front of me, I won't mind" he said as he lies down on the bed and put his one hand under his head.

I groaned.

"But I do mind. Forget it, I'll change in another room" I stated.

"You know what you change here. But soon you'll not feel awkward in front of me whether you are in clothes or not" He said the last line more to himself and left the room.

I stood there for few minutes blushing with my racing heart.

I ran towards the door and locked it and hurriedly grabbed a dress and wore it.

I was in no mood to do make-up so I skipped it as I was not going anywhere today.

Be sure that Eros didn't get scared away.

I rolled my eyes.

Then exited the room and went to downstairs to make my tummy full.

When I reached downstairs I found Eros sitting on the dining table doing something in his phone.

I walked there and asked him what is he doing?

"Oh you're here, please make some breakfast for us, I'm really very hungry" he replied.

Is he mistaking you as some chef?

"What? Why would I? Where are the staff members?" I asked.

"Honey, If someone was here then why would I ask you to do so?" He said.

Did they got scared by your no make-up look?

Shut up.

"Where are they?" I questioned.

"My mom gave them a day's off so they won't disturb our romance as you know we're newly married couple" he said with a wink.

"Oh right, but there is a problem that I don't know how to cook" I embarrassingly said.

"You're lying no? Because if you're joking, this is not a right time for your humor " He stated.

"Nope, I seriously don't know. What will we both do now? Do you seriously don't know how to cook?" I asked.

"Nope. Let's make something together. What you say?" He questioned.

"Alright. We can try and take out is always in the list" I smiled.

I hope the kitchen didn't end up turning on fire.

We both reached the kitchen and started making something.

After few attempts of cooking and almost burning it down we decided to spare the kitchen, so we both decided to order food.

And we finally did our brunch when the food came.

After eating he gave me a tour of his house sorry, our house and I came to know he's having a library, a theater room, a play room(not like Christian Grey's room but an actual play room with different games) and a boring office. The house also have a backside pool. I really wanted to swim in it but the major problem is that I can't swim.

And I don't want him to see me like an duckling who's trying to swim.

A funny duckling.

Shut up!

After taking a tour of the whole house, we ordered dinner without even thinking of trying to burn up the whole place.

After eating the dinner I went to bed and he went to his office.

I know these CEO and their obsession with work.

Who do the work on your second day after marriage?

You're saying like that you want him to be with you all the time.

It's not like that but he can spend his time with me and we can know each other well, I don't know anything about him except that he is rude, arrogant, conceited and annoying,

Okay, we got your point.

I ignored my stupid thoughts and went to sleep.

After don't know how much time the door open and he came.

He sat on the bed as I can feel the mattress dip, he pulled me closer to himself and kissed my lips and said good night.

I was half asleep so I didn't protest him to let go of me and honestly speaking, I was too comfortable in his arms so I let him hold me and with that I was in my dreamworld.

Thank you thank you thank youSoooo much for liking the story.

It's all because of your support.

Keep on supporting my story.

Please do vote and comment.

Love you all soo much

12/04/2018

Chapter 26

- -

S carlett's clothes above

Scarlett's POV

It's been four days since I got married to Mr. Rude aka devil aka my husband.

He was not much rude to me as he was busy with his second wife.

No not any mistress or any lover but none other than his office.

Are you getting jealous?

I scoffed. Why would I be? He can do anything, as if I care.

Today Eros was at home but in his office and I was sitting in front of television searching for something interesting to watch.

You can always watch your face in the mirror. Such a great piece of art.

Shut up.

Suddenly the door bell rang.

Who can it be?

For that you have to get up from your throne and move your legs and walk towards the door leaving your lazy ass behind.

Hey! Don't be mean, I was going to do that.

When I opened the door there stood a Victoria Secret model, with perfect blonde hairs, long fake eyelashes, brown eyes. Her aura was yelling bitchy. She wore a tight red dress which shows more of her body than it was covered.

I got interrupted when she clicked his fingers in front of me.

"Hey you, move out of my way and why did you take so much time to open the door" She stated and pushed me away and started walking inside.

What the hell?

"Bring one glass of orange juice for me?" She ordered looking at me.

What? What is she thinking of me?

May be she mistook you,

Yeah, I think you're right but this is no way to treat someone like that. She's a meany.

"Sorry I'm not the one you're thinking" I fake smiled at her.

"Oh.. so who are you if you're not a maid and what are you doing in my baby's house?" She asked arrogantly.

What? Baby?

I didn't knew that this house is owned by a baby.

Last time I checked this was Eros's house.

"I didn't get your name " I asked.

My mouth was aching because of this stupid fake smile.

"Because I didn't tell you" she scoffed.

Please do one thing for me.

What?

Kick her ass out of the house.

I really want to do that. But at least let me know who is she.

"Hey Tara, you here? You should have told me about your visit. I would have received you by myself" Eros said by coming from my behind and hugging that girl named Tara.

Why do I get a feel like she's a bitch.

Same with me.

"Honey meet my friend Tara, we both were in the same school and we both are the famous ones" he said by winking at her.

I forced a smile onto my face.

"Nice to meet you Tara" I fake smiled.

"But who are you honey?" she asked a bit more politely according to my consent.

What? Is She bipolar?

"Tara she's my one and only beautiful wife Scarlett" Eros told her by giving me a side hug.

"Oh so she's the one?" Her face showed disappointment and disgust.

"I didn't think that you'll marry a girl like her" she said by looking at me in disgust.

"No worries she's beautiful" she completed with her famous fake yucky smile.

I really wanna clap my hands with her face within my hands.

"I think I must go now, I have done booking in a hotel as I don't have any place to stay" she said looking sad which I also found fake.

Really?

"Oh no no, you aren't going anywhere. You can stay with us I know my wife won't mind a guest" Eros told her.

I'm hating him for doing this.

Now I want to punch him in his face.

"Really I can stay with you? I mean in this house?" She cheerfully said.

Her intentions are not good.

"Of course you can stay here, now come I'll show you your room. You go and get some rest then we'll meet at dinner " he told her.

I wish I don't ever see her.

"Okay as you say, thanks Scarlett for letting me stay here" she cheesily said.

But when did I agree?

But I didn't got a chance to say anything as they both left the living room. I took a deep breath to calm my nerves.

May be she isn't that bad.

And may be you're wrong.

I also left and head towards our room with a big sigh.

When I entered someone grabbed my waist and pulled me.

The same intoxicating cologne came to my nostrils.

"Thank you so much Scar, for letting her stay here." He said with a kiss on my lips.

When did I? But, who cares?

Obviously, you.

Hush.

"It's your house you can invite whosoever you want" I replied.

He glared at me but soon continued.

"She's a close friend from my childhood, her father is was father's friend, so we lived our childhood together. We also dated each other but it didn't work out. So we both moved on our lives and now she's here" he said remembering his memories.

So they have dated each other. Why did I felt pang of jealousy within me?

I sighed.

"So you both are just normal friends now?" I questioned.

"Yupp, nothing else. You should feel secure. Your husband isn't leaving you ever" he teased.

"I don't feel anything for you so you can do whatever you want" I replied.

He raised his eyebrow and gave me an 'are you serious' look.

I just shrugged.

"Okay then, you won't mind if I hug her like this" he said by tightly embracing me.

"And this" he kissed my neck.

"And not to forget this" he kissed my lips.

And this kiss fully melted me. All my anger flew away. His touch erupted sparks inside me. He traced his hands on my back.

I'm wearing my clothes but I still feel like his hands were on my bare back.

He was kissing me like there's no tomorrow. He slowly slowly moved towards my cleavage with all the soft kisses.

But the door of our room burst open.

Why always someone interrupt your special moment? I want to file a case on this matter.

The person who interrupted us was none other than,

Tara.

The bitch.

I tried to pull myself away but Eros didn't let me.

Her face was showing anger but she soon changed it like it wasn't even there.

But why would she be angry if she sees us like this. After all we are married.

"Tara I think you should knock first before entering someone's room" Eros scolded her.

I tinge of happiness ran inside me.

Kiss him for me.

"Um.. I'm sorry Eros but I just lost and your room's door came and I barged in."

She said shooting daggers at me.

And kick her for me.

"It's okay. Next time please knock before entering" he said.

Add hug with the kiss.

"Okay, actually I'm feeling hungry so, can we have dinner?" She asked.

"Yeah it's time for dinner. You go downstairs we'll soon join you" he dismissed her.

"When will you come Eros?" She asked only to Eros like I wasn't even standing there in the same person's arms.

Hello Ms. Bitch I'm also here.

"Tara you can very well see that I'm busy with my wife. So please excuse us" he said like he's controlling his anger.

Eros let go of that anger don't stop it and kick her also fake ass out.

She nodded and left.

"Sorry for her" he said.

I smiled.

"It's okay, you don't have to say sorry for her" I said.

"I'm not saying sorry for her but for the interruption in our kissing. But no worries we'll continue this later " he said with a final kiss on my lips.

I blushed and he chuckled.

I ran away from the room as fast as I could.

As this rate you'll soon get slimmer.

What is he doing to me?

We all got seated on the dining table and ate our dinner. I wish I could say peacefully but because of this chatter box, I can't even eat properly.

Eros left the table as an important call came. So now we both were eating.

"How did you trap him?" She said.

"What?" Is she talking to me? I glanced around me.

Stupid you see any one else here?

"Don't act dumb I know he can't marry someone like you, so what did you do? I know him very well he'll not marry a girl so down standard like you? So you whored around him?" She asked.

I was stopping myself to kill her with the knife in my hand.

Babe.

Shut up. Don't you dare stop me.

But?

Shush.

Listen?

Zip it.

Scarlett?

What?

The knife you're using is a butter knife. You can't kill her with that.

Oh!

I kept it back.

Let's win the fight with words.

I cleared my throat.

"Listen I don't do whoring around like you, so don't even dare to compare myself with you. And I was not the one who wanted this marriage. It was Eros himself, he came to me and asked me to marry him. And as you know now he's my husband so keep your dirty ass away from my husband. Because he's mine and he belongs to me"

Bravo, I love you for this.

"Oh really, I came back to do take my Eros from you. He was always mine. You came between us and this time I'm not going to leave him" she said by standing up with a punch on the table.

I also stood up from my seat and crossed my arms.

Yeah why would you sit when she's standing.

"Do whatever you want to do because you are not getting him, nor now or ever. He now belongs to me as he's my husband. Don't you dare lay an eye on him because I also don't know what will I do if your fake body came in my hands. So stop whoring around my husband" I stated by pointing my index finger towards her.

With that I left the table and went to my room and slammed the door shut.

How dare her for saying all that bullshit to me. I'm not going to leave her.

She thinks that she'll take Eros from me but I won't let that happen, he's mine.

What? Now you are declaring that he's yours. So you love him now?

It's not like that, um.. I don't love him, but he's my husband and I should save him from that fake material.

Yeah and I'll do that.

I took a shower and wore my nightwear and jumped into the bed.

I was deeply thinking about how to make that bitch leave my house when I felt something soft on my shoulder.

When I looked at it Eros was showering kisses on my shoulder.

Can't he see I'm busy in a serious thought.

"I thought you're asleep" he said by trailing kisses to my neck.

"I'm awake, so now let go" I whined.

I tried to push him but it's of no use.

I groaned and tried to bit him. But he dodged me.

I huffed.

"Aww, my wifey is getting wild day by day. Now you wanna bite me" he teased.

I blushed and hid myself under the duvet.

He laughed.

"Come out wifey you know I want you in my arms to sleep" he said.

"No I'll sleep like this tonight" I told him.

"So you're not coming out?" He asked.

"No.."

"Okay then I'm coming in and I don't know what'll happen when I'll get to cozy with you " he said.

I quickly came out of the duvet and heard his laughter.

"Now be a good wifey and come in your too damn hot and sexy husband's arms" he said.

I rolled my eyes but I did as he said.

What? I feel comfortable in his arms. As you know he's my husband I can do that.

With that we both fell into deep slumber hugging each other.

Pheww

Chapter completed.

I hope you all like it.

What do you feel about the new character?

Keep on voting and supporting.

14/04/2018

Chapter 27

Scarlett's POV

Next day when I woke up I found the bed empty, I climbed off the bed and searched for Eros but he was nowhere to be found, I huffed in annoyance. Why he have to leave me so early in the morning? ugh.. Mr. Rude.

But where did he go?

Aww, such a loving wife you are.

I postponed the search of Eros and decided to take a hot and steamy bath, if he doesn't care so why would I? I took a bath and brushed my teeth and wore something comfy and exited our room.

When I was walking down the stairs I heard gales of laughter from downstairs, curiosity rose in me and I ran towards the sound of laugh.

Is there a comedian came? May be that Tara brought someone like her. Please go there asap I don't wanna miss anything that is funny.

When I reached there, I saw Eros, Nick and the fake assed girl aka Tara laughing.

I think that fake ass girl is a comedian that's why they all are laughing.

When I reached there their laughter died down and they all turned their attention towards me. I greeted everyone good morning with a smile,

But Tara ignored me by ignoring my gaze.

"You're awake babe" Eros said with a kiss on my lips which made a frown landing on Tara's face.

Ooo someone is annoyed by you,

"Morning shortcake, so you're happy with him or regretting your decision of not marrying me?" Nick teased,

No way, Eros is best. She was jumping all time that Eros married her.

Shut up, when did I jump?

I'm your inner voice and I know when you're jumping when you're not.

"She's happy with me and I'm glad that she selected me, so Nick stop flirting with my girl and find your own" Eros replied giving me a side hug.

My girl, start your blushing session Scar,

Hey! I don't blush that much.

Yeah and water isn't wet that much.

I shook my head and gathered all my attention on their childishness.

Aren't they so cute.

"My bad" Nick said by putting a hand on his heart showing fake hurt.

I rolled my eyes, I was about to reply to Nick when Tara interrupted me,

"Guys, today's weather is amazing so why don't we all go to the beach, what y'all say?" Tara excitedly asked.

What is going on in her micro mini mind?

I bet that that something is evil just like her.

"I think that's a good idea" Eros said with an unknown glint in his eyes.

Now what is he thinking?

I wish I can read people's minds.

Then may be you'd be less stupid.

Wait a minute.

No you can't, you'll still be stupid.

Shut up.

"Fantastic, I'll see some hot chicks there showing their beautiful body, Ah! I can't wait, let's get going then" he dreamily said.

I rolled my eyes at his comment, why all the boys are like this?

"We'll leave for the beach in an hour so get ready everyone" Eros said by clapping his hands.

I walked back to my room and took out the bikini which Sonya bought for me and told me that a girl must have a sexy bikini with them, who knows when it will be needed. And now I think she's right.

It is a really sexy black colored bikini with criss-cross straps in the front. When I wore it I can't help but to admire that bikini on my body, I wore it beneath a white T and blue shorts. I tied my hair into a messy bun and took my sunglasses, sunscreen and some necessary items and put it into a bag and wore my slippers. I didn't wore any make-up because I don't want it to smudge and make me look like a raccoon, so with a little lip gloss I was ready to go. I grabbed the bag and exited the room.

When I reached downstairs everyone was there except Eros.He came a few minutes after me.He was wearing denim shorts and a white T and white sneakers. He was looking so young and handsome in that boyish attire, how did I get so lucky?

I also think the same most of the time, like how?

When he looked towards me he stood on his spot and checked me out from up to down then a smirk makes its way on his face,

I blushed.

"Wow, you two match. Typical love birds" Nick teased.

Right, we are matching, oh! That's why he was watching me like that.

"Let's get going now. We're getting late, Eros you coming?" Fake ass purred as she was walking closer to Eros not forgetting to sway her fake ass.

I really wanna puncture that ass.

I hurriedly walked towards him before that fake ass bitch reaches him and pulled him towards me by holding his forearm and started walking towards the entrance. Eros didn't argue but I can see his shocked expressions but that soon turned into an satisfactory smirk. When I glanced back at that bitch she was shooting daggers at me. What can I do, she was trying to take my husband.

And you're feeling jealous.

I'm not.

Keep on lying to yourself.

When we reached the car I thought I dodged her but she was walking beside me trying to beat me. Is she a magician or a great runner? She was behind you, right?

She tried to sit in the passenger seat with Eros but I beat her and got seated next to him. Yes! She was left with no choice but to sit on the backseats.

Well done Eros's wifey.

I smirked at her in the rear view mirror. Bitch.

Eros sat on the driver seat smiling at me and Nick sat beside Tara at the back but an annoyed expression was on his face and he was glaring at Tara, guess I'm not the only hater Soon we were off to the beach.

Whole ride that Tara tried to make conversation with Eros, sometimes praising his body or forcing Eros to relive the moments of their college life so that I can feel left out but Eros didn't let that happen, he kept on asking me about my views or about my college life, and when he held my hand in his, Tara stopped making anymore conversation.

Ha! Take that bitch, he's not available.

I exited the car when we reached the beach. A goofy smile appeared on my face, I can smell salty and fresh air, the sounds of waves reached my ears, I took a deep breath.

Hey control, otherwise you'll steal whole earth's oxygen.

Hey I'm an normal human,

I wish you were.

Shush, let me enjoy it.

The beach was not crowded as always, a few people were there. I don't like to be in a crowded area. Today is really a best day to be at a beach. Awesome weather plus less people.

That's good few people will see your fat body.

Hey! I'm not fat.

Alright, don't scare me.

Eros and Nick took the matts and the bags out of the car and we all left in the search of a perfect place to sit. Soon we found it and we all got seated on the matts.

The atmosphere was so calm so amazing, but the calmness soon got disrupted as The bitch aka fake ass girl started removing her clothes looking at Eros with an disgusting expression.

Eww. Is she trying to seduce him with that expressions?

I don't think anyone's going to be seduced by that expressions, they are creepy.

She was wearing a skimpy yellow bikini covering.. not covering, exposing everything, her tanned body. Her figure was good but I can't say that she's the rival.

Yellow yellow dirty fake assed fellow.

She kept on sending that creepy looks towards Eros totally ignoring me. I cleared my throat but she just kept on looking at Eros. And most importantly Eros wasn't even looking at her, he was busy in doing something with his phone. I don't think that he had seen her nothing covering bikini. I'm proud of you Eros.

Let's dig a hole and bury her down in the beach but with her fake ass up.

I chuckled. That's a great idea.

"Eros would you please put the sunscreen on my body?" She seductively asked. Can't she see he's not interested at all.

Such a fake assed seductress.

"Nick will do that as I have an urgent call to attend, Scarlett I'll be right back" he told me and with that he left without even sparing a glance at her. I did a happy dance in my mind.

That's what you get when you eye on others husband.

An ear to ear grin appeared on my face and Nick saw it. He chuckled at my reaction.

When Nick asked her to do that she snatched the sunscreen from him and said she don't want to apply it anymore.

She really wanted Eros to touch her. Thank God he didn't do that. Then we have to wash his hands with acid.

Nick shrugged and came to me.

"I see you're happy that Eros is not sparing a glance at her. He knows who matters in his life and who don't, you know? This Tara is a pure bitch or witch whatever you wanna say since the college years. I never liked her" he said.

She knows magic, damn, she can make you more uglier.

I frowned. Hey I'm not ugly.

Um.. yeah.. but she can make you.

"Why are you saying this? Is she also trying to get your boyfriend?"

He laughed.

"You're so cute Scarlett and FYI I'm totally straight as a ruler and I like girls, hot and sexy girls. I was not talking about me. She's you can say kind of obsessed with Eros, she was once his girlfriend but that didn't go well so Eros dumped her but she's so clingy, she tried so many times to make him hers but it didn't happen, so be careful with her" he warned.

Bloody husband stealer fake assed bitch.

"Eros don't know about her stupid obsession with him?"

"He knows that she like her but of obsession, no he don't. I know he's a bit crack" He said.

I also agree.

"That's true, he's truly oblivious to her tactics" I murmured but Nick listened and laughed lying on the matt.

I flushed.

"Thanks for the warning. I'll take care of that bitch and save my cracked hubby" I winked.

He grinned as he lied on his back, with his shades on. His both hands were under his head.

"So how's your friend Sonya doing?" He asked from nowhere.

Sonya?

Is anything cooking?

Stupid Scar, we're on a beach not in a kitchen.

I rolled my eyes.

"I haven't talked with her since marriage. She's busy with something. But why are you asking?" I interrogated.

He shrugged.

"No reason, I just found her beautiful and cute... oh shit" he covered his mouth, he cleared his throat before continuing " I mean she's a good girl and indeed a good friend and she's your bff so uh I think uh I'll join you later" with that he went to swim.

I chuckled, he's so cute. I removed my flip flops and sat on the matt. I closed my eyes to feel the calming effect of the waves and the wind when I felt someone sat beside me. I peeped by opening an eye and found Eros sitting next to me. He was already looking at me with a smile. I opened both my eyes and kissed him on his cheek. But I unfortunately turned my face towards the shore, where was the world's no no, century's worst view. Tara came out of water with her skimpy bikini which was tightly clinging to her. She was walking seductively glancing at Eros, swaying her hips perfectly so that she can look sexy.

I know she's sexy, why god why? You should've made the exes ugly not hot and sexy, Ugh. I ignored her and turned my face towards and found him already staring at me.

Wow he didn't spare a galnce at her.

"What?" I asked trying to hide my blush from his scrutinizing gaze.

"Did you bring your swimming costume?" He asked.

"Yup but why are you asking?"

"Then show me your sexy body babes" he teased.

I rolled my eyes.

"After you honey" I said by fluttering my eyes and gliding my finger on his T shirt covered chest.

"I didn't knew that you are that desperate to see me naked. I know you love my abs but baby you just have to ask and I'll be naked whenever you want" he seducitvely said.

His abs came into my mind which turned my cheeks pink.

He chuckled. But soon he started removing his clothing slowly one by one in a teasing manner.

My blush deepens and I lowered my gaze.

I heard a roar of laughter from him. When I glanced back at him he was only in his swimming trunk. Nothing up nothing down. I audibly gulped.

Cover him woman, that fake ass girl is roaming around.

"Now it's your turn. Let's see your body can stand in front of me or not" he challenged.

I raised my eyebrow but started removing my clothes slowly and seductive-ly. I can feel his intense gaze on me. When I turned my face towards him he was gawking at me.

I smirked.

"So what do you think?" I questioned.

"Perfect" he mumbled under is breath while gawking at me up to down. He was constantly staring at me. I clicked my fingers in front of his eyes.

"Back to earth dream boy" I said.

He cleared his throat.

"Scarlett you're looking so.." Nick said while coming back to the sitting area.

"Hot" Eros completed.

I blushed.

"Yeah.. you're right man. I truly regret that, why didn't she met me first, Scarlett you should've bumped into me. I can be a good wall, wanna try" Nick said.

"No Nick, she won't and your bad man because she's mine" Eros said coming closer to me and kissing my forehead.

"Atleast think of the singles, some people don't have their lover beside them and they don't come bumping in your life, anyways I'm going to get a drink" Nick left with a fake sad expression.

We both chuckled.

"Honey don't you think you're bikini is kind of short and exposive, it doesn't cover much. I can see your stomach easily " he said looking at me.

Seriously?

"Eros it's a bikini and it is like this" I told him.

"Why don't you wear your clothes back. I don't like to let other people see what's mine and you're looking too hot in this" he said by roaming his eyes here and there.

Possessive much. But I like it.

When I looked around most of the guys were starting at me and some girls are shooting daggers towards me. So I did the only thing that came in my mind I hugged him, to tell everyone that we both are booked. I sat down on the matt and starting putting sunscreen on my body.

"Do you want me to put sunscreen on you?" Eros asked.

"Yeah sure" I replied.

His hands roamed all over my body. I was finding it difficult to stop my body from shuddering under his touch. After applying the sunscreen we both were seated side to side.

"Can I kiss you?"he asked.

"What?" I asked raising my eyebrow.

"Um.. nothing, forget it" He said.

"Yes" I told him.

A smile formed on his face. I came closer to his lips and on instinct he closes his eyes... Perfect.

I threw sand on him and ran away giggling.

That's awesome. Now run for your life.

When he opened his eyes, he said "Run baby" and he ran after me.

I laughed but continued to run.

When I turn around he was not there. Where did he go?

Suddenly I was in the air, lifted from the ground and was on a shoulderI squealed.

Same cologne came to my nostrils.

Eros.

I tried to wiggle out of his grip but no use. He then smacked my butt,Oww.. I yelped.

"Stay still" he said chuckling.

Hey babes, nice ass no?

I smacked his butt and said, "keep me still"

He shaked his head chuckling.

He took me to the shore and threw me in the water. I landed with a splash, I was coughing badly but was shooting daggers at him.

He was laughing at me.

Everyone around me was laughing. But the fake ass was showing annoyed expression.

I ignored her.

I asked him for help. When he gave me his hand I pulled him but instead of him falling I fell down again with a splash.

Stupid idea from stupid Scarlett.

Eros laughed this time clutching his stomach. He looked cute while laughing like this, so carefree. I splashed the water on him. His laughter died down. I quickly ran away but being me clumsy I again slipped and fall down in the water again.

"Why are you so clumsy?" He said within his laughs.

I wish I knew the answer.

"Come here" he said and helped me to finally stand on my feet. I lowerd my gaze getting embarrassed of my clumsiness.

"Don't be embarrassed I like your clumsiness" he said with a peck on my lips, which soon turned into a passionate kiss.

"Oh my virgin eyes" Nick interrupted us by covering his eyes.

From no where Tara came and snatched Eros away from me.

I huffed. I'm gonna kill her.

"Told you" Nick shrugged.

I controlled my anger and enjoyed a few minutes with Nick.

He's a nice company but not when you're angry. He'll make you pull your hairs and become bald.

I really want to see a bald Scarlett.

We left the beach and head towards a restuarant where Tara sat on the right of Eros while I sat on the left.

I once again stop myself to puncture her fake ass.

We ordered our dinner and soon the dinner came and we all dig in.

Fake ass was getting very touchy with Eros. I gritted my teeth.

Soon a hand came on my thigh and I choke on my food.

"Hey are you okay?" Nick asked.

I nodded.

Eros was smirking at me.

I narrowed my eyes at him and put my hand on his thigh.

Which made him choke on his food.

I giggled at his condition.

"What is happening with both of you?" Nick again asked.

"Nothing" Eros and I said in unison.

Tara was shooting daggers at me. But I shrugged and ate my food. Why ignore this delicious food for some fake silicone girl.

Soon we left for home. Nick left for his house and Tara.. nothing. I was totally exhausted to go to my room. Eros came behind me and lifted me up in his arms and headed towards our room.

I didn't forgot to smirk at Tara who was killing me with her dangerous look.

Bitch, I'm the wife.

I'll soon throw you out of our house. I promised to myself.

This chapter was soooo long

Pheww

I hope you all like it.

Keep on reading and supporting.

15/04/2018

Chapter 28

Thank you all sooo very muchFor liking the story.

Enjoy the chapter

~~~□~~~

Scarlett's POV

When I woke up I was tangled up with Eros. His one arm was under my head and another was on my bare tummy my top must have ridden up while I was sleeping. I was in my pj shorts and a tank top. Our legs were badly tangled. I tried to get myself free from him but he didn't budge.

I groaned.

What is he? A giant? A caveman?

Or are you even trying hard?

I tried to push him in result I fall off the bed with a loud thud on my bums. Ouch!

I groaned.
~~~

Why did I told you to try hard?

I think I broke my bums. I rubbed them.

I believe you because you know the hips don't lie.

I rolled my eyes.

"What happened? What are you doing on the floor so early in the morn-ing?" Eros asked in his sexy morning voice.

Shit. What would I say to him. I can't tell him that I fell.

Say that you have an urge to kiss the floor or something like that.

"Um.. I was doing, um.. yoga.. floor yoga, yeah, floor yoga" I told him.

Bravo! What an excuse.

"What? Then why are you rubbing your bum?" He frowned.

Damn.

"Uh, I am doing rubbing bum aasan" I told him.

Is that even an aasan?

Don't know.

"What?" He confusingly asked.

"Uh..Nothing, forget it" I hurriedly got up and left for the washroom.

I can hear his laughter from outside.

Why are you so clumsy plus stupid plus the worst liar?

I don't know.

I did my business and took a nice bath and wore a knee length light blue comfy dress.

Eros was smirking at me after I came out from the bathroom. He took a shower and exited when I was standing in front of the mirror.

"Now I know how you maintain your sexy body" he said looking at me in the mirror.

You have a sexy body? Since when?

"How?" I frowned.

He came near and whispered in my ear.

Is he going to scream in your ear.

Shut up.

"Because of that unique yoga of yours" he teased.

He's smart.

I blushed hard. My cheeks turned pink so covered my face with my palms.

He laughed.

"I again want to see you doing that aasan" he teased.

Yeah.. only if he new that how much the bum hurts.

True. I can still feel the pain. After getting dressed up we both went downstairs for the breakfast and luckily fake ass was not at home.

I think it's your lucky day. Enjoy babes.

I happily did my breakfast without seeing that plastic model.

Soon Eros left for his office after doing the breakfast. Not forgetting to kiss me before he left.

Now you can do whatever you want, even you can yell like tarzan. No one will see you.. but you already yell like tarzan.

I ignored my inner voice.

I watched TV as I don't had anything to do.

Soon the front door opened, and the fake ass came but her expressions turned into a scowl after she saw me sitting on the sofa.

I think her face is like that.

May be, I chuckled.

"Who are you laughing at?" She questioned.

Obviously you, duh. Can you see anyone one else here. Dumbo bimbo.

"Oh nothing it's the series I'm currently watching in which a girl, no.. no a bimbo... yes. She tried hard to snatch someone's husband by doing different things but instead of that she end up on the streets when the wife kick her butt out of the house. Such an amazing series. Right?" I told her.

"What do you mean by all this? Why are you telling me this stupid story?" She asked confusingly.

I sighed.

"I thought you have more brains than that. But I was wrong. Are you seriously so dumb to not understand what I'm trying to tell you?" I asked.

I can see her face getting red from the anger. I can literally see the smoke coming out of her ears.

Ohh! Finally she understood you.

"How dare you? You bloody ugly bitch. What do you think of yourself that you are so beautiful and innocent? No you're not. I don't know what Eros see in you. You think that your dear husband will choose you instead of me? No chance. Have you ever seen your face? And not to forget I'm his old friend but you're nothing but a gold digger who married him and doing some kind of dirty tricks on him. You think that he'll support you," she laughed her evil laugh.

What a bad laugh she has. I think Nick's right that she's a witch. True evil witch.

"You're wrong bitch. Because he'll select me over you. You just came a few days ago. There's no chance of you. I suggest you to grab your bags and leave him before he threw you out of this house and you become the one who lands on her butt" she said by crossing her arms.

I had enough now.

What does she thinks of herself? She is such an ugly bitch. She thinks that she can yell at me like I'm her slave and I'll not reply her back.

She's wrong, totally wrong.

Tell her babes where does she stands.

"You? Eros will choose you over me? Huh? Never. What do you think of yourself? You bloody psycho stupid bitch. That everyone in this world die for you, for your fake ass and your fake plastic body. You're wrong there. No one is going to die for you. You skunk. You are staying at my home like you're the queen. Treating everyone like a crap. You're nothing but a useless weight on the Earth. You think I'm a gold digger, have you ever seen yorself in the mirror. You ugly bitch. If you have looks which I don't think so you have, that doesn't mean you'll crush everyone. Your looks are just like you fake. And it's not me who is going to leave this house. You're the one who'll soon be leaving this house. As this house is mine. Don't even try to put your dirty self on my husband otherwise I'll kick that fake ass of yours so hard that I don't know where will you land" I hissed.

Well done. Amazing. First time in your life you did something that good.

"But why are you saying like that Scarlett. I know you don't like me but don't say like that. I really respect you. Why would I try to snatch Eros from you he's my friend I don't wanna loose him? Don't accuse me for that low thing" She replied by flowing fake tears.

What happened to her? Why is she behaving like a victim?

Whatever. I don't give a damn about it.

"Accusing you for such low thing" I laughed.

"Darling you're a low ugly creep who can make one's like living hell. And for liking, yeah I don't like you at all I hate you. Your bitchy nature, your fakeness, sometimes I think you're a whore who...." I was interrupted by a familiar sound.

"Enough" Someone said more like yelled.

Who dared to stop you in middle?

When I turned around Eros was looking here with fury in his eyes. His face was red and I know he's fuming in anger.

Yippie, your night in the shining armour came.

Yess. Now the bitch will know to whom she was messing with.

"What's going on here?" He asked angrily, he was looking so scary. A shiver ran through me at his cold look. Thank God it's not for me. I crossed my arms and a victorious smirk formed on my face.

Now she'll know who's the boss.

"Eros she was accusing me for so low things that I want you and was snatching you from him by whoring around you. Why would I do that? You know me do you think I'll do that to you? I know we're friends and I don't want to loose a good friend as you." she said by flowing alligator tears.

Little she know that her tears won't work on him.

I chuckled to myself.

"I didn't said anything wrong Eros. You know she's a bitch and who knows how much she'll stoop low.." I was cut off in mid.

"Enough Scarlett" he yelled.

At me.

My eyes widen from shock, I stared at him in confusion. Why is he yelling at me?

My heartbeat speeded.

I think he mistaken your name with her.

He came forward and stood in front of me, towering my petite frame with his giant body.

"I never expected this from you. You are accusing her for such low things? I knew her and I don't think she'll do anything like this. But Scarlett you, you were never like this, you were so innocent so soft spoken so kind. Where did that Scarlett go? Or was I mistaken? Is this your real side. Were your soft and polite behaviour was acting?" He yelled.

I flinched when he yelled at me. My eyes were wide open. Refusing to blink.

How dare he? He believed that cunning bitch?

My vision blurred. He's accusing me for a thing I never did. He didn't even tried to know the whole thing. How could he?

He don't believe me. Is she right that he'll choose her over me. Was I expecting much. That he'll be on my side.

I audibly gulped and controlled my tears and spoke with the remaining strength left within me.

"Eros you're getting it all wrong. I'm not the one to whom you should yell at. I didn't do anything wrong. Believe me she's the one who tried to snatch you away from me. She wants to take you away.."

"Stop it Scarlett. I know you don't like her. And why would she do all this when we both knew that nothing worked out between us" He stated.

"But Eros" he stopped me by raising his palm in front of me to stop.

I really want to punch his beautifully sculpted face.

A traitor tear left my eye which didn't go unnoticed.

With that tears started flowing on its own. He don't wanna believe me. He's accusing me without even knowing who is wrong and who is right. Here I thought he'll believe me but he believed her. He believed that girl who is a bitch disguised as a friend. Someone said it right that don't expect anything from any one. He proved it right. I was a fool to believe that he'll prefer me over her. I think there was nothing between us. We both were just playing the roles that our mother wanted from us. This marriage will always be a forced marriage. No love is going to happen between us.

I looked at Tara she was smirking at me telling that she's right that Eros will believe her. She was right, I was no one. So why would he believe me. He knows Tara before me. May be I'm not meant to be here.

Eros you're going to regret this.

I stood there numb. Everything inside me feel broken.

"Eros please don't yell at her it's not her fault. She felt insecure that's why she said all that. You both knew each other for a few days, may be she doesn't trust you that much. She should have trusted you. I don't want to create more problems. I think I should leave you both" with that she ran away from the front door.

I think she had done masters in acting. Stupid Bitch.

Eros was glaring at me still annoyed. I moved forward but he stepped back.

"I was wrong about you.." he left after saying that calling Tara's name and that was my breaking point. I fell on my knees. All strength was evaporated from me.

I was wrong about you...

I was wrong about you...

I was wrong about you...

It kept on repeating in my mind.

I groaned at the numbness. I can't feel anything other than that stupid pain that I don't know where's happening. My whole world crash down. I felt like I'm broken. I was totally numb.

I sat on my knees and cried for don't know how much.

I feel broken.

Something snapped in me. If he doesn't want me so I'll leave. He don't trust me so he can live his life happily with Tata. I can't stay like this forever, I stood up and went away from the house without glancing back.

Yeah, you don't need him. Let him believe whosoever he wants to believe. He'll regret in the future.

If he doesn't believe me let him be then, I can't do anything for that. I walked and walked don't know where.

I don't need you Eros when you don't even trust me.

I was right.

You are Mr. Rude.

And you're not mine.

What do you guys think? She'll leave Eros or Eros will make up with her and see the reality of Tara?

To know?

Keep on reading guys

17/04/2018

Chapter 29

E ros's POV (I hope you missed him)

I came office after having breakfast with Scarlett.

She was quiet when she ate. I am happy for that.

She's really so sweet and caring. I'm glad that I married her.

She's sweet when she's quiet but when she opens her mouth.. God knows what happen to the precious ears of the people.

She don't speak that much.

Really?

Okay. She speaks a lot.

Now I was going back as I forgot an important file in my office at home.

I'll able to see Scarlett once again.

You're seriously badly whipped.

I drove back to my home.

When I entered the front door yelling noices came from inside.

Is wrestling going on inside or some yelling competition?

When I came closer I see Tara and she looked at me.

"But why are you saying like that Scarlett. I know you don't like me but don't say like that. I really respect you. Why would I try to snatch Eros from you he's my friend I don't wanna loose him? Don't accuse me for that low thing." She said to Scarlett.

What? Is Scarlett seriously accusing her for that? I can't believe it.

What's going on in here? Why are they yelling and why is Tara saying all that?

"Accusing you for such low thing" Scarlett laughed.

Look.

She continued.

"Darling you're a low ugly creep who can make one's like living hell. And for liking, yeah I don't like you at all I hate you. Your bitchy nature sometimes I think you're a whore who...." but I cut her off in the mid.

Seriously what happened to Scarlett. She's not like this.

I can't take it anymore. What happened to Scarlett? Why is she accusing Tara for such things.

"Enough" I yelled.

Both of them turned towards me.

"What's going on here?" I asked angrily.

I was angry, angry would be an understatement, I was furious.

Calm down and listen to them first.

Scarlett looked me with hope in her eyes whereas Tara was happy to see me.

Scarlett is happy to see you.

"Eros she was accusing me for so low things that I want you and was snatching you from him by whoring around you.Why would I do that? You know me do you think I'll do that to you?" Tara said as her tears started flowing.

I don't believe her. Scarlett can't accuse anyone like that. I don't trust your friend here.

Scarlett said all that? But why?

I didn't think that she'll accuse Tara my friend for such a thing.

Hey don't jump on conclusion like that. May be Scarlett's right.

I can't believe it but why would Tara lie?

"I didn't said anything wrong. She's a bitch and who knows how much she'll stoop low.." I again cut her off.

"Enough Scarlett" I yelled.

She flinched.

She's even accusing her in front of me. I felt hurt. Scarlett was not like that as I thought.

"I never expected this from you. You were never like this, you were so innocent so soft spoken. Where did that Scarlett go? Or was I mistaken. Is this your real side. Were your soft behaviour was acting?" I yelled.

Hey don't jump on conclusions like that. May be Scar was right.

I'm really feeling bad that I chose her. She looks innocent only from face but inside she's not like that.

How could I mistook her as innocent.

I have a feel that she's innocent. Can't you see it in her eyes.

"Eros you're getting it all wrong. I'm not the one to whom you should yell at. I didn't do anything wrong. Believe me she's the one who tried to snatch you away from me. She wants to take you away.."

Eros believe her for me. I know she's right.

I had enough now.

"Stop it Scarlett. I know you don't like her. And why would she do all this when we both knew that nothing worked out between us." I stated.

I saw Tara was crying badly. Poor Tara.

She's not poor.

"But Eros" I stopped her by raising my palm in front of her to stop.

A tear flowed down her cheek. My heart swelled looking at her like that.

She started flowing tears. I felt bad that they were because of me. But what can I do she was wrong this time. I can see hurt in her eyes. I can't see her crying. I controlled myself. I felt pity on Tara. She was being accused for such thing.

I'm surely gonna hate you for making hrr cry.

"Eros please don't yell at her it's not her fault. She felt insecure that's why she said all that. You both knew each other for a few days, may be she doesn't trust you that much. She should have trusted you. I think I should leave you both" Tara ran away from the front door.

I have to comfort her.

No, you should comfort Scarlett. What happened to you?

I was still glaring at Scarlett when she raised her hand to touch me but I stepped back.

Her eyes now show pure hurt.

Am I doing something wrong in not believing her?

Yes you're doing wrong. And I'm sure you'll regret it later on.

"I was wrong about you.." I said and left the house after Tara.

I don't wanna talk to you. I'm going. Bye.

I found her seated on the front of the house.

She hugged me. I had no other option so I hugged her back to comfort her.

You should have comforted your wife. But why am I talking to you?

I thought you were gone.

I was but I can't leave you alone with this Tara.

I took her to one of my hotel so she can relax. I can't take her back to my home.

Yeah then she'll say rubbish to Scarlett.

This time you're on wrong side.

You know? I really don't wanna talk to you.

We reached the hotel room and she went to washroom. I ordered someone to bring her clothes from my home.

I lied down on the bed thinking that why did Scarlett do such thing?

No she didn't but you didn't believed her.

Now you're talking?

I can't shut my mouth that's the main reason and when you're doing stupid things I have to tell you.

Why are you supporting Scarlett when you also have seen her accusing Tara for all that rubbish?

But you entered in the mid, you haven't heard the whole conversation. May be Scarlett was right. You very well know how Tara is.

A few minutes later the bathroom door opened and Tara came in room wearing nothing but bathrobe which was loosely tied to her.

Is she sad? From where? I can't see her sadness.

"Are you okay?" I asked her.

She nodded and hugged me.

I tried to pull away but she didn't let me. She started roaming her hands around me. Soon she started showering kisses on my body.

If I have Scarlett in my life. I would be glad to do so. But now I feel like I'm cheating on her.

It felt wrong. I felt disgusted. I pushed her away.

She stumbled back.

"Tara, stop it. You know very well that I'm married. I can't cheat on my Scarlett. She's still my wife. So be in your limits" I turned my face away from her.

Thank God atleast you remember that.

"What does she have that I don't have? I'm more sexier than her, more prettier. She has nothing. She's an ugly bitch. She don't deserve you." She said.

"Then who deserves me? You?" I asked.

"She have everything that I want to be in my wife and you know very well I like you as a friend, nothing more will happen between us. She deserves me more than anyone else." I stated.

"Why? Why can't you love me like her? I did everything that I can do to get you back. I waited for you for years. But when I came to know you married someone. I got mad and came here as soon as possible. Why can't you look at me like you look at her? Eros atleast try I'll surely make you happy than she makes you" she requested.

"I can't, I just can't cheat her. She's is my wife I will never ever cheat on her and you know we can't be anymore than friends" I told her.

"You'll be only mine Eros. You know how much I have done to make you mine. I tolerated that shit of your wife, I'm the one who provoked her to say all that. I knew that's the only way you'll hurt her. She thought that you'll choose her over me. Stupid much. Huh! But I broke her thought. She never deserved you. She's a gold digger nothing else. She whored around you and trapped you..." I shutted her up this time.

How dare she say all that about Scarlett. I told you she's right but you didn't listened to me not even Scarlett. Are you going to slap Tara or may I?

"Enough Tara. Don't you dare say a single word about my wife. I chose you over her that's my worst mistake. All the time when she was begging for me to listen to him she was right. But I chose friendship over my wife. How can

I be so dumb that I chose you over my wife, my Scarlett? How could you Tara? I thought we were good friends" I was on the urge to broke down.

Bro.. you screwed up big this time.

I accused my Scarlett for a thing that she never did. Her eyes were showing the truth but I chose to ignore her. How stupid am I? How will I get her back?

I thought she's stupid but you beat her this time.

"I don't want to be your friend because I love you Eros. Please forget that bitch and come to me. We're perfect for each other. We'll be so happy in our future. Forget that ugly bitch" she said by coming closer to me.

I pushed her away.

"Tara everything's over between us. I don't want to have any connections with you. You're dead to me. I don't wanna see your face in my whole lifetime. Just get lost from my life " I huffed.

With that I left the hotel.

How will I get my Scarlett back? Will she forgive me? I hurted her. I can see how I crushed her under my stupid decision. I was really stupid to believe Tara when my heart was telling me that she's right.

Oh God!

Just apologise to her. I think she'll forgive you.

But what if she didn't? I can't live without her.

Think positive man.

I drove back to my home praying all the time that she'll forgive me.

When I reached there, the front door was open. I yelled for Scarlett but no one was there.

May be she was in another room.

I checked the whole house but she was not at home.

Did she left me? Will she never come back?

I can feel my whole world breaking down. I felt broken.

I fall on my knees.

I hold my head with both my hands.

Where is my Scarlett?

Will she come back?

What have I done?

Poor Eros

What do you guys think?

Will Scarlett come back or leave Eros?

Keep on reading to know further.

Do vote and comment.

Love you all

19/04/2018

Chapter 30

E ros's POV

I was sitting on the floor for don't know how much time.

Thinking about my Scarlett.

Will she ever come back to me?

What have I done?

I should have listened to her instead of that bitch of a friend.

Suddenly my phone goes off. When I look at it Nick's name shows on the screen.

I really was in no mood to talk to him and listen to his stupid talks.

Pick it up. May be he'll help you.

I received it after few minutes of thinking.

"Where are you?" he yelled in a deafening voice.

"At home. Why?" I asked totally not interested.

"And do you know where's Scarlett?" He questioned.

That catches my interest.

I frowned.

"No. I dont know where did she go. I am waiting for her to come back home. Nick I screwed up big this time." I replied.

"Calm down man, she's here at a bar where coincidentally I am also present. Just come here asap." He said.

She's at a bar? Is she alright?

"Is she alright Nick? Is my Scarlett fine?" I asked.

"Yeah man she's fine. Just come here fast" he said and hung up the call.

I got up and ran towards the bar whose address Nick send me, where my Scarlett is.

I exited my home and drove towards the bar.

When I reached the bar I hurriedly enter the bar and searched for my Scarlett.

Instead of Scarlett I found Nick. He came towards me.

"What have you done this time? Because I was literally not able to control her. First time in my life time I was not able to control a girl." He said.

Because my Scarlett is different from any other girl. She's unique and she's mine. But what happened to her? Why was Nick not able to handle her?

Yeah I agree totally unique and don't forget she's the stupid Scarlett, whom everyone can't handle.

"Nick I'll tell you everything later. First tell me where is she?" I asked now getting restless.

He told me where is she by pointing a finger in a direction.

When I looked at that direction. I saw her. Sitting on a stool and talking to the bar tender.

I released a breath of relief.

I walked towards her. She was busy in talking to bar tender, she didn't notice my presence.

What is she talking with him that she didn't notice you?

"Scarlett..." I started.

She turned her face towards me. When she recognises me her eyes widen and I can see the hurt in them.

I felt bad.

You should.

"I hate you " she slurred and turned her face towards the bar tender.

Me too.

Wait?

Is she drunk?

I again called her instead of replying me she said " please tell him to leave me alone and he can go to the fake assed girl" to the bar tender in a slurry tone.

Fake assed.. Lol, but she's right. She's too damn drunk. Hilarious.

He chuckled at her words. But turned towards me with a serious expression.

"Man you can leave her she don't wants to talk to you. I think you should go" he said.

How can he say that to me?

Because he have a mouth..duh.

I gritted me teeth.

"She's my wife so I would say that to you to leave her alone" I hissed at him.

"Whoa man, I didn't knew that. Hey sweet cheeks why don't you talk to your husband by own" he said.

Exactly, why need a mediator.

"I would have done that but this guy standing here beside me is a very bad husband." She said

I'm with her in this.

Traitor.

"You know he's Mr. Rude, he's always rude with everyone not everyone only me. Even he yelled at me but there was not my fault, still he yelled at me. Infact he chose those fake asses over me" she said whispering all these to the bar tender but her voice was not at all a whisper.

I shaked my head.

What can I say she's drunk and a person doesn't become intelligent after drinking.

Bar tender shrugged.

"I think you should listen to him, may be he has his reasons for that." He said.

"You're supporting Mr. Rude, I'll also not talk to you" she huffed.

I smiled at her. She is looking so innocent and cute.

"Okay okay I'm sorry I won't support him but you have to stop drinking" he said.

She scrunched her nose but nodded.

I sat beside her, she glared at me but soon continued talking to bar tender.

She thinks you're boring. So she decided to ignore you.

"Hey shortcake how's it going?" Nick came and asked her.

"I was good but your friend beside me made me bad " she said.

Why are you so bad Eros?

Whose side are you at?

You know my answer.

I know you'll be always with me.

Obviously hers.

What the hell man!

"I'm sorry Scarlett. I didn't know that Tara was after me, it's all my fault that I chose her over you. Please forgive me princess " I apologised.

"What man? You chose Tara over her. Are you mad or what? If I was Scarlett I would have kicked your ass right there" Nick said.

You really need a kick on your sexy ass.

I glared at him. He's not helping me at all.

"I know Nick I was wrong and now I want to apologise for all that. I promise you princess I won't ever repeat that again" I said.

"Why would I believe you that you won't do that again?" She questioned.

Exactly.

Shut up.

"I'm promising you princess, just give me a chance" I said.

"And if he did something like this again my arms are always open for you shortcake" Nick said by opening his arms dramatically.

I smacked his head which caused Scar to giggle.

"Ow man.. have mercy on my beautiful head " he said rubbing his head.

"I'll forgive you if you kick that fake assed bitch out of the house" she said.

Nick chuckled at her.

You had already done that.

"Oh baby I have already did that, she's no more staying with us" I said.

She smiled her cute smile.

"Which means I don't have to see her fake ass" She excitedly said and jumped from her seat to hug me.

I hugged her back.

Same here. I think her hair was also fake. Don't you think?

"Hey let me also join you. I also don't like her and I'm also happy" he said and hugged us.

Perfect moment.

"Can't...breathe" she said and we all pulled away.

"Now let's get you home "I said to her.

"Let's take Nick with us, what if someone came and teased him. And I'm leaving who'll save him. Poor Nick" she innocently said.

Nick and I both laughed.

She's damn cute.

She's so caring but not to forget stupid too.

"Don't worry shortcake. I'll save myself from world's evil eye" he winked at her.

She grinned.

I got up from my seat and asked to get up but she said that she don't wanna walk so I should lift her, which I gladly did.

Because she's not a fatty giant that's why you can lift her.

She giggled and said goodbye to Nick by kissing him on his cheek. Which obviously made me jealous.

We both exited the bar and made her sit in the passenger seat of my car and got seated on the driver seat.

I looked at her and she giggled.

I knew she's mad but didn't thought the time will come soon to send her to asylum.

I rolled my eyes.

Then we both drove off to our home.

We reached the home and I told her to come out.

"I don't wanna walk, I want a ride to my room so lift me up please" she said.

I shook my head at her cuteness.

I lift her up and walked towards our bedroom.

I made her sit on the bed and went to closet to grab her as well as mine clothes.

I brought one of my shirt for her and wore my sweatpants.

I heard someone singing.

Who wants to make me deaf?

When I came to room I saw Scarlett was jumping on the bed and singing song and holding a hairbrush as a mike.

I laughed at her.

Please somone tell her to not to sing in her whole life. I don't want to see people deaf.

When she saw me she instantly stopped which caused her to slip and she fall on the bed.

I laughed out loud this time.

Stupid plus clumsy.

She blushed and covered her face with hands.

She then got up and started unzipping her dress while hopping like a rabbit.

What is she trying to do?

"Can you please help me in removing this, I want to wear something comfy." She said.

Oh! She has some unique ways removing a dress.

I unzipped her dress and turned around and gave her my shirt.

She took it and when I turned around after few minutes I saw her struggling to get her hands out from the sleeves.

She's too small for my shirt.

Obviously man, she's a mice in front of you.

But she looks damn hot, my shirt suits her more than me. I can see her sexy legs.

I have to control myself. I can't do anything as I don't want her to regret in the morning.

She pouted then head towards the washroom.

I was about to lie on the bed when I heard a scream and Scarlett came out running.

She collided with my chest which made us fall on the bed. She was on the top and I was beneath her.

"What happened? Are you alright" I worriedly asked.

"No, I think I saw a spider inside the washroom" she said hiding her face in my chest.

Poor spider.

I chuckled.

Oh God why's she making it hard for me to control.

"It's okay princess. The spider isn't going to eat you up" I said her by firmly holding her waist.

"What if the spider bit me and I became a spider women. I don't wanna be one" she said.

Seriously? I didn't expected her to be this dumb.

I laughed so hard that my eyes watered.

"Oh baby why are you so cute?" I said between my laughs.

She frowned.

Soon she gets silent.

When I see her she was watching my lips.

"Can I kiss you?" She asked from nowhere.

With pleasure.

And who am I to stop her. I smashed my lips onto hers.

She moaned in pleasure. I can't control myself now so I rolled on my side which made me on top of her.

I was kissing her madly. I really love her lips. They are a way that takes me to heaven.

I broke the kiss and moved downward to her collarbone. I kissed her sweet spot which made her moan.

My hands automatically reached towards the hem of the shirt. I pulled it upward and touched her bare soft stomach.

I can see that she's enjoying the kiss as she was moaning my name.

"Eros.. I need you" she moaned and sat on top of me and started unbuttoning the shirt.

I can't do this to her now when she's not in the right state. I want her to remember every detail of our first night.

I stopped and pulled her, which made her fall on my chest.

I can see the disappointment in her eyes.

I stroked her hair.

"Not today princess. I want you to remember everything of our first night. So now sleep" I told her and kissed her forehead.

Soon her breathing calm down which means she's asleep.

"Sleep tight baby" I said and soon drifted off to sleep with Scarlett on top of me in my arms.

----

www.ingramcontent.com/pod-product-compliance
Lightning Source LLC
Chambersburg PA
CBHW071423200726

48294CB00002B/499